NOT HIMS[...]

He pressed the mask against his face and looked at the mirror.

Milo whined. Stanley turned and saw the dog dive under the bed.

Then things got very strange indeed.

Tendrils of wood shot out of the edges of the mask and wrapped themselves around his head like tentacles. He grabbed at his head and then suddenly, inexplicably, he began to spin. Like a top. Slowly at first, then faster.

"Helllllpppmmeeeee!"

Panicked, Stanley reached for the bedpost, grabbed it.

The spinning stopped, cold.

He took a couple of deep breaths. He looked down, saw a smoking trail burned in the carpet.

He lurched back into the bathroom and looked at the mirror.

The miror revealed an apparition that made his dragon landlord look like Miss America. His head was green, bald, bug-eyed and had a rictus that revealed tombstone-shaped teeth three times normal size under a boney, beaky nose.

THE
M·A·S·K

Steve Perry

Based on the screenplay
by Mike Werb
Story by Michael Fallon and
Mark Verheiden

BANTAM BOOKS
NEW YORK · TORONTO · LONDON · SYDNEY · AUCKLAND

THE MASK

A Bantam Book / August 1994

*Grateful acknowledgment is made for permission to use the lyrics from
"Gee Baby, Ain't I Good to You." Music by Don Redman. Lyrics by Don Redman &
Andy Razaf. Copyright © 1929. © Renewed 1956 Michael H. Goldsen, Inc.
© Renewed and Assigned 1985 Michael H. Goldsen, Inc.
Owned 100% World Wide by Michael H. Goldsen, Inc.*

ISBN 0-553-56929-5

Published simultaneously in the United States and Canada

*Bantam Books are published by Bantam Books, a division of Bantam Doubleday Dell
Publishing Group, Inc. Its trademark, consisting of the words "Bantam Books" and
the portrayal of a rooster, is Registered in U.S. Patent and Trademark Office and in
other countries. Marca Registrada. Bantam Books, 1540 Broadway, New York, New
York 10036.*

PRINTED IN THE UNITED STATES OF AMERICA

OPM   0 9 8 7 6 5 4 3 2 1

For Dianne, again.

In masks outrageous and austere
The years go by in single file;
But none has merited my fear,
And none has quite escaped my smile.

—*Elinor Wylie*

THE
M·A·S·K

PROLOGUE

THEN

A cold gray wave slapped at the dragon's head. Icy spray and foam spewed past the guardian carved into the wooden prow, drenching Eriksson yet again. He ignored the wetness and the seaweed stink, having grown all too used to it.

The longship fell into the wave's trough, and men cursed as their bellies churned from the sudden drop. Thick fog gripped the little ship like a clammy hand as it had for days, and yet again, Leif, son of Erik the Red, wondered if perhaps they weren't close enough to the Edge of the World finally to jettison their terrible burden. The ship moved sluggishly with the currents, the square sail flaccid under the dead gray sky. How could the seas possibly be so choppy with no wind? What cruel joke were the gods up to now?

The gods, he had come to realize, had a crappy sense of humor.

The deck lurched under him and even with sea legs months in the making, he fought to hold to his feet. All right. Odin had not given them an easy task. He laughed aloud. When had it ever been so?

One-eyed Olaf sloshed his way across the ankle-deep and slippery deck toward Leif, doing so with care. To do less was to risk joining the five men who had already been claimed by the gods on this hell-ish voyage.

Olaf, however, had not reached the advanced age of nearly forty winters by being careless. One did not get to be an old Viking by falling into the bone-freezing sea.

"No wind," Olaf said, by way of greeting.

"Oh, really? I had not noticed." The sarcasm was lost on Olaf.

The old man blinked his single eye, then rubbed at his wet beard. He stared out into the fog. "Per-haps we should bend to the oars?"

"Old friend, have you really risked the entire length of the ship to tell me these things I already know?"

Olaf shook his head. He turned to face Eriksson. "Leif, we must be nigh onto the Edge by now. Can we not do the deed and turn back?"

Eriksson knew how the old man felt—it was the mirror of his own thoughts—but it was not seemly for a leader to show any weakness. He shook his head. "Nay."

Olaf said, "Our crew is near mutiny."

Eriksson turned a cold gaze upon Olaf. For a long moment he did not speak. When he did, it was calmly, with no anger. "The first man to say such a thing aloud will follow his head into the depths."

Olaf nodded and sighed. "I thought as much. No harm in asking."

Eriksson and Olaf both looked at their cargo. The box: the box that was both bolted and chained to the deck. A box as heavy as Thor's hammer. The ship could upend and roll onto her back and that box would not move. The wrist-thick oak planks of the container were bound in seven fat strips of iron, seven being the proper magical number, and the heavy bands then sealed with molten brass, accompanied by the prayers of a dozen priests and two witches. Eriksson put more faith in the iron bands than in the prayers, but then, he was a simple man whose sword had gotten him out of more trouble than magic ever had. The box had been designed to stay closed and right where it was until it reached the Edge of the World, and reach there it would, unless some catastrophe claimed the longship on the voyage. And even so, the damned contents would go to the sea bottom with the ship, did that happen. It had all been so arranged by those much wiser than he.

Leif the Lucky, they called him. It was why he had been chosen for this trip.

He shook his head. Had he *really* been lucky, *another* would have been given the odious task.

To Olaf he said, "We sail until we can sail no more, old friend—"

There came a drawn-out crunch! Many oaths were uttered.

The longship ground to an abrupt halt. Eriksson and Olaf sprawled to the awash deck, as did most of the other sailors.

More colorful imprecations resulted.

Kloss the lookout picked himself up dripping from the deck. "Uh, land ho?" he called.

Eriksson came to his feet and wiped the fishy bilge water from his beard. He glared at the lookout. Kloss was a slackwit. Kloss made a ship's rat look like a wise man. Kloss was too stupid to pour piss from a boot.

"Fool!" Eriksson yelled. "You are supposed to warn us of land *before* we run aground upon it!"

Kloss shrugged. "Ah. Sorry, Cap'n."

Well. Eriksson shook his head in disgust for the ten thousandth time since the voyage had started. Expecting the entire crew to be lost because of the nature of the trip, the Elders had not given him the cream—save for Olaf, who was a decent warrior, his one eye notwithstanding—but rather the dregs of the Vikings. Kloss, bad as he was, was not even the worst of them. Fortunately, the worst two or three had been among those who had fallen into the sea and been lost. Eriksson still held hope that Kloss would soon join them. And at times he had been tempted to speed up the event—

A sudden wind sprang up, and under its touch, the fog cleared somewhat.

Land, sure enough. And a large chunk of it, too. *Thank you, Odin.*

"The hillside yonder is covered with berry vines," Olaf said, pointing.

Eriksson nodded. This . . . vineland was not how he envisioned the Last Place before the Edge of the World. Which surely it must be. With the fog burned away, the country was actually quite appealing. A quick foray had shown them much greenery, decent rivers, plenty of game. The snow was sparse, even now in the winter. Were the place not about to be cursed by what they had come to do, it would have been a good country to settle in. Too bad.

"Almost done," Kloss said from behind them.

Eriksson turned. They were not far from the breakers, on a sandy stretch of beach. He saw that the hole was as deep as a tall man was high. Nodded. "Do not fall in. And fetch the witch," he said.

Two of the men scurried away.

Eriksson turned to look out to sea and, as he did, heard the startled yell and thud as Kloss fell into the hole he'd just helped dig. He sighed. *Why me, Sweet Odin? How did I offend thee?*

The others helped Kloss from the hole as the witch came nigh.

She was, on the face of it, beautiful. Dressed in a fine blue-and-white robe and most exotic looking, the witch was smooth of cheek, heavy of breast, with strong, sturdy thighs that looked to be able to put a fair grip on a man. But no sane Viking on the longship, no matter how long the voyage nor how pent up he might become, would risk touching the witch. The guise she wore was beautiful, but it was false, and her true features would turn a vulture's stomach inside out; they knew, they had seen her now and again when her magicks had slipped. To lay a hand on the witch would cause that hand—or any *other* part of himself a man might extend toward her—to wither like a leaf in a hot flame. A thought to sober the drunkest man.

"Be quick about it, witch," Eriksson said.

The woman smiled, an expression warm enough to melt copper. She pulled a scroll from beneath her clothes and unrolled it. The crew had all been wet so long as to grow mold on their clothes, and yet the witch had a dry parchment under her pristine garb. That should be clue enough for even a stupid man that she was not quite human.

Kloss smiled at the witch and licked his lips suggestively.

Eriksson shook his head in wonder. Kloss was in a league of his own when it came to stupidity. Given the way the gods had been doing things of late, Kloss would likely survive the voyage to become rich and fat, to die of old age in bed surrounded by dozens of grandchildren.

The witch spoke. "O ancient Loki, thy mischief, which was bound and contained by seal and sound, is now given unto this ground. May you sleep forever in the earth of this place!"

The witch mumbled several more phrases in a tongue Eriksson did not know. As she did so a sudden wind arose and began to kick up sand. It howled across them, plucked at their clothes, tried to shove them back into the surf.

Dark clouds boiled up from nowhere, built skyward into towers of purple and gray, shot through with bolts of lightning and the rumble of thunder.

Hail began to fall, stones as big as a man's own. The hail swept across the beach and began to pound upon them.

Some of the men held their shields up over their heads, those who had thought to bring them ashore. Eriksson raised his own shield. The unfortunate warriors who had left their protection on the ship covered their heads as best they could with their hands and arms.

The clatter of the hail grew louder. The stones grew bigger.

"Ow! Ow!" The men danced around, as if doing so would keep them from being hit. A fist-sized hailstone smacked Kloss on the head and bounced high into the air. Eriksson doubted that a boulder of ice would affect Kloss, whose head must surely be solid bone.

"An omen!" Kloss said. "Ow! Ow!"

Eriksson stared at him. Leave it to the idiot to voice what all could see.

"Witch!"

She hurried through her recitation, rolled the scroll up, and tucked it away. "Done!" she said. Eriksson could not help but notice that none of the hail fell upon her.

"Do it!" Eriksson commanded.

The men shoved the box into the hole and began to shovel the dirt and sand over it. Burying it was the work of but a moment. They were in a big hurry.

A lightning bolt struck the ground nearby and the thunder blasted them. Men screamed. Was Thor angry with them?

"Back to the ship!" Eriksson screamed above the din.

The crew ran for the smallboat at the water's edge.

As they ran, the hail falling and the lightning cooking the land around them, Olaf yelled at Eriksson: "You're the captain of the ship that discovered this place, Leif, will you name it?"

"Not I! Our people will never return here, it is cursed forever. Leave it for the Swedes. Or better, the Italians. Let *them* name it."

"Ow! Ow!" Kloss howled.

Leif, the son of Eric, ran for his ship.

NOW

The fat woman waddled along the beach lugging her giant beach bag and her umbrella, scream-

ing at her five children as they ran for the water.
"Watch out for glass! And hypodermic needles!
And don't go out too far!"

Billy, Susie, Sandy, Joanie, and Bobby ignored
her and ran flat out for the dark gray-brown murk.
Even the foam on the surf was that color, although
it was a little lighter than the water itself. Kind of
reminded her of how shoe polish foamed when you
put it on a shoe.

The fat woman shuffled her two hundred and
forty-seven pounds along the sand, glad she had
worn her flip-flops, 'cause the sand was *really*
scorching.

Behind her, the skyscrapers of Edge City
loomed, the smog thick enough to blur them into
hazy impressions. Too hot to stay in town, that was
for sure.

The beach was packed, even on a weekday. Not
many places left. She worked her way among the
sunbathers, looking for an empty spot. Finally she
saw one and made for it. She noticed another family
heading that way, but she hurried, waving them off.

"Hey, we saw it first!" a thin woman in a bikini
said as the fat woman thundered in, barely beating
them.

"First *come*, first served, dearie."

"Hey, lady, if you move over just a little, we can
share—"

"Piss off."

She spread her blanket—actually it was the old
red-and-white-striped sheet that Susie had puked
on that hadn't come clean in the wash—and stuck

the beach umbrella up in the sand, right next to the
big sign.

The sign said, BEACH CLOSED! RAW SEWAGE. NO WAD-
ING OR SWIMMING.

Everybody knew that unless you swallowed the
water or something, it wouldn't hurt you, so nobody paid any attention to the sign.

She smeared sunblock on her face and shoulders, put her dark glasses on, and pulled the big
radio out of her bag. She turned the radio on. The
disc jockey on the radio said, "Yessirree, it's a hot
one out there today, folks! We are wieners on God's
barbecue, french fries in the devil's boiling grease
pit. The weather bureau is issuing a third-stage
smog alert. No rain in sight. Fluorocarbons are up,
the Dow Jones is down, and oh yeah, the killer bees
have finally arrived from Mexico! Another beautiful
afternoon here in Edge City. Great day to go to the
beach!"

The music began to play. The King, singing
"Don't Be Cruel."

Some smart-ass kid two blankets over turned his
boom box up, that gangsta rap crud. The fat woman
twisted her volume knob and drowned out the
sound. Hey, Elvis had sung about ghettos long before these rappers had come along. These kids
today, they didn't have any sense of history. The
King had soul before any of them were even born.
There would never be another one like him. Never.

Maybe she would take the kids to Graceland
again this year. If Harold could get his vacation.

Her kids splashed around in the surf along with five or six thousand other children. She didn't worry, there were lifeguards here somewhere; plus no sharks or anything could live in the water this close to shore, that's what the news said.

Just past the surf line was a big industrial barge with DEPARTMENT OF SANITATION printed on the side in big letters.

The fat woman stared at the barge and rubbed more lotion on herself.

The diver saw the remains of the box as he ran his dredger back and forth under the cracked sewage pipe. The pipe was bigger around than a pickup truck, and the struts on which it sat were in pretty bad shape, substandard construction like all the rest, which was why he was down here anyhow.

He didn't like to swim under the big steel pipe, but that was the only way to get a good look at what he'd unearthed from the bottom muck. And he'd better do it if he didn't want Louie to spot it and beat him out of it.

Hmm. It looked like rotted wood with bands of pure rust around it. Some kind of symbols on the box, too. He held his lamp on it while he tried to pry the rusted metal away from the box. Christ, this thing musta been here for hundreds of years. Maybe it was pirate gold or something.

He looked around. Louie was on the other side of the pipe, he couldn't see him. Well, if this *was* pirate gold, by God, it was his. He found it, he was

going to keep it. He managed to dig through the
rotted wood enough to get good leverage. The stainless-steel knife, a quarter of an inch thick across the
spine, popped the rusty bands easily.

Bubbles came out as the box began to open.

Hot damn!

He got a quick glimpse of something as the box
fell apart. Crap, it didn't look like gold or jewels.
Whatever it was, it floated out of the shattered box
in the bubbles, started to rise toward the surface, he
couldn't get a good look at it—

Above him, the pipeline shifted suddenly. He
saw the strut break. Had just enough time to look
up and scream into his mouthpiece as the pipe fell
and crushed him against the bottom. He thought he
heard somebody laughing and then he didn't hear
anything as it all faded to black—

The fat woman washed partially melted bites of
a half-pound Hershey bar down with sips from a
can of diet Coke she'd brought. The Coke had gotten a little warm, but that was okay. The deejay
came back on the radio. At the same time a helicopter with the Channel 6 News logo on it swooped
down from the swirly brown sky toward the barge
and began to hover over it.

The deejay said, "Word of a terrible accident has
just reached us. A Department of Sanitation diver
has been killed while working on a broken sewage
pipeline off Vineland Beach."

The fat woman sat up straighter and looked at

the barge and helicopter. She rummaged around in her beach bag and pulled out her Watchman TV, flicked it on.

Yep, there it was, the view from the Channel 6 helicopter.

She plugged the TV earphone into her ear and turned the radio down. The Channel 6 reporter was talking.

"—yes, Bill, we're here at the scene. A Coast Guard boat is on the way."

"Kathy, do we know the identity of the dead man yet?"

"No, Bill, not yet."

The fat woman hunched over the Watchman, trying to keep the screen in deeper shadow. Oh, boy. A dead diver. How interesting.

There was a loud boom. The fat woman looked up, startled.

The sky was filled with dark clouds. Lightning flashes and more thunder rolled across the water and beach. Where had *that* come from? There wasn't any rain in the forecast!

People began packing their gear. The thousands of children in the water ignored the sounds of the lifeguard whistles. Parents began screaming for their offspring. It sounded like a riot. Like a dying dinosaur or something.

The fat woman shook her head. Well, crap. The day was ruined. If she had to stay inside the house with the *children* all afternoon because of the rain, she might go crazy.

Well . . . crap!

She forgot all about the dead diver as she hurried to pack her bag. She yelled for her own kids, slurring all of them into one word: "BillySusieSandyJoanieBobby!"

Bobby, the baby, came running up first.

"Momma, Momma, look what I found."

It looked like some kind of wooden mask, slimy and dirty and probably covered with sewage—and God knew what else. "Go throw that nasty thing back in the water!"

"But Momma—"

"Do it right now! It's gonna rain and we have to get to the car! Go on!"

Bobby went.

These children. They'd pick up anything.

Thunder rumbled.

1

Stanley Ipkiss stood between his desk and Charlie Schumacher's, staring at the stupid sign next to Charlie's name. They all had that sign on their desks somewhere: WE BANK ON TOMORROW. Stanley's was artfully buried under his in-basket, which, since it was always full, kept the sign out of sight. Not that it mattered: the vault, right behind his desk, had a banner over it with the same stupid slogan, in foot-high letters. Well, of *course* they banked on tomorrow—*every*body banked on tomorrow. How many people got up in the morning and said, "Well, I think this is my last day on Earth"? Really. Edge City First was not only hidebound and stuffy, it was too cheap to hire an agency; instead, they let the chairman's idiot son write the ads. And his other idiot son ran this branch of the bank. It sure paid to choose the right parents.

Charlie's parents were good people, but his father had been a small-time salesman, hawking encyclopedias before he retired to live on his Social Security. And his mother had never held a job outside their little home in the suburbs.

Charlie stared out through the first-floor window. A distant rumble of thunder rattled the glass. Rain began to patter against the window, big fat drops. You could smell it, even through the air conditioner, that wet, dusty odor. Maybe it would cool things off a little. It was body temperature out there, at least. He'd gone out on his break to get a soda— the bank was too cheap to supply coffee for its employees—and almost cooked on his way to the magazine stand on the corner.

Pedestrians on the sidewalk ran for cover.

"Hey, it's supposed to be another hot day in Hell Town, where'd that come from? Idiot weathermen can't find their asses with both hands. Run, you suckers!" Charlie said.

Finally, he looked up and saw Stanley.

"Well, hello, manly Stanley. 's up?"

Stanley shook his head. Charlie was thirty-four, a few years older than he was, and also a bottom-rung account exec. He was, in his own mind, at least, a lady-killer and man-about-town, too. But he'd been in the same job for nine years, a prospect that didn't make Stanley real happy, since Charlie was senior, and should a promotion ever open up, he'd get first crack at it.

The way things were going, he might be in this job until he died of old age—

"Manly Stanley?"

Spaced out again. Stanley shook his head and sighed. "Don't call me that, Charlie. How would you like it if I called you Charlie . . . ?" He trailed off. The silence stretched long as Stanley realized he couldn't think of anything nasty that rhymed with "Charlie."

When he got right down to it, he couldn't think of *any*thing that rhymed with Charlie. Come on, Stanley, *think . . . !*

"Charlie is good," Charlie said. He grinned. "What can I do you for?"

"We're supposed to go over these stats, remember?" He waved the inch-thick sheaf of printouts. The guys on the second floor had laser printers, but here in the Dead End Kids' department in full view of the bank's lobby and front door, all they had were two wheezy antique dot-matrix units with bad ribbons and half the pins bent or missing. They'd had three, but a paper jam last week had caused one of them to burst into flame and melt into plastic slag. Most exciting thing to happen around the place in months. Maybe years.

"We're supposed to have a complete report before lunch, remember? That's lunch *today*."

Charlie took the printouts. His eyes went wide as he tried to read the faint and skewed impressions on the sixteen-pound perforated-edge paper. The

paper itself was so cheap it still had little chunks of
pulpwood in it.

"Jesus." He tossed the paper back at Stanley.
"I'll go blind. I'll have to buy a white cane. A dog
that craps all over my apartment. Cut me a little
slack, Stanley. I was up all night watching a newly-
wed couple in the building across the alley and I'm
a zombie, it's all I can do to breathe. Be a pal and
take care of this, Stanley. I'll owe you one. Hell, I'll
owe you two. C'mon."

Stanley stared at the seated man. He should have
known. Charlie did this to him all the time. Charlie
the . . . Barley? The Harley? The Gnarly?

There must be *some*thing. Charlie the . . . ?

Shoot. He should tell Charlie to put the printouts where the sun didn't shine, *that* was what he
should do. Tell him he was tired of carrying him, of
doing all the work whenever they were supposed to
be collaborating! Tell him to do his *own* damned—

"Stanley?" said a voice made of silk and honey,
spiced with hormones that would make a hundred-
year-old monk's interest rise.

He turned and saw Maggie standing there. Maggie the teller beautiful, who was twenty-six, blond,
green-eyed. She had blood-red fake fingernails an
inch and a half long, wore a white blouse and a
miniskirt that stopped halfway between her knees
and her . . . well, short enough so when she bent
over, there was no doubt about the color of her underwear.

No doubt whatso*ever*.

He forgot all about Charlie. "Uh, hi, Maggie."

"Hi, yourself. What?"

"Huh?"

"You wanted to see me," she said, raising one eyebrow.

"I did?"

"You left a *note* on my counter, Stanley."

"Oh, oh, yeah. I—I—ah—got those tickets. For the MegaPuke concert on Friday." He reached into his black sport-coat pocket and pulled the pair of tickets out with a flourish. "Ta-da!"

Maggie lit up. What a great smile. Probably her parents had put some orthodontist's kid through Harvard or Yale for those teeth, but it was worth every penny. "You *did*? That's great!" She reached out and took the tickets, looked at them. "Wow! I heard they were all sold out!"

"They were. I have, uh, connections."

Yeah, connections. A scalper who approached him on the sidewalk outside the ticket office. He'd had to hock his stereo to cover the cost of these suckers, but if Maggie would go out with him . . . well, it was worth that, too.

Stanley's heart raced. This was actually going to happen. She *was* going to go out with him. He was blessed. The gods had smiled on him. It had been a while, too, and about time.

The last woman he'd taken out had been Betty, a waitress at the diner where he used to eat dinner a couple of times a week. She was forty years old, forty pounds overweight, had bad breath, and it had taken him six months to work up the nerve to ask her to a movie. She'd agreed and he'd been thrilled.

The thrill didn't last. The date with Betty had been a disaster, like every other date he'd ever had. She'd demanded he take her out for dinner before the movie, to a "nice place," and he'd dropped eighty bucks feeding her. At the movie—a Schwarzenegger picture she wanted to see because she liked men with muscles and not skinny little shrimps like Stanley, not to be insulting or anything—she'd consumed a tub of popcorn and a large soda, a box of jelly beans and a large box of Junior Mints. During the funny parts of the movie—a lot of parts, even though it wasn't a comedy—she laughed like a demented hyena, causing people to turn around and stare at her. She gave them the finger when they did.

Finally, at the door to her apartment, she'd burped in his face, giggled, and said he should call her again, she'd had fun. She shook his hand, left him standing on the stoop. At a hundred bucks a date, Stanley figured he could afford to take her out maybe once every six months, so he'd stopped eating at the diner where Betty worked and started going to McDonald's instead. He had to stop answering his phone for three weeks because she called every night wanting to know where the hell he was and how dared he trifle with her affections like that? She was, she'd said, seriously considering suing him.

But here Maggie was, smiling at him, a dream and not a nightmare. "So, what time should I pick you up? I mean, do you want to go out and eat first, or whatever?"

She frowned.

"Something wrong?"

She sighed. "Well. See, my best girlfriend—ah, Susan?—just came into town and she's dying to go to this concert. Could you, like, you know, get another ticket for her?"

Stanley's bowels turned to ice. So much for the smiling gods. They had a . . . lousy sense of humor, the gods. "I don't think so. There aren't any more tickets to be had."

"Oh. Oh, dear. Well, see, I can't just let her stay home alone on a Friday night." She looked around, then leaned down confidentially. She had to lean down, as she was a good six inches taller than Stanley in her heels. She said, "Her fiancée just broke up with her, you know."

"Oh. I see." He didn't see what that had to do with MegaPuke at all, but it seemed like a safe thing to say.

Maggie looked at the tickets. Shook her head. Sighed. Held them out toward Stanley. "So, I guess, well, I guess I can't go."

She looked so sad. Like her dog had just died. Like her house had burned down.

Like she wasn't going to get to go to the Mega-Puke concert.

Well . . . crap.

He said, "No, keep them." He smiled, hollow
and full of pain and managed to say, "Take your
friend."

"Oh, I couldn't do that." But she pulled the tickets back and stared at them hungrily. Like a starv-
ing woman with a crust of bread.

Like a lioness protecting a bloody zebra steak.

"No, no, go ahead. I don't like concerts that
much anyhow. There's all that . . . music and all."

Lame, Stanley, lame, lame, lame.

But it didn't seem to matter. The tickets vanished into her pocket. Poof! She was good. Maybe
she was related to Houdini.

"You are so sweet," she said. She looked at
Charlie. "Isn't he the sweetest man? Sharon will be
so thrilled!" She gave him an air kiss, then turned
and swayed off, the high heels and short skirt just
as interesting from the rear as they had been from
the front. He watched her return to her station with
mixed emotions.

"As much as I would like to have a swing like
that in my backyard, *that* was disgusting," Charlie
said. "Sickening. It is to hurl. Bleh."

Stanley blinked. "What are you talking about?
What was I supposed to do?"

"Do? *Score*, that's what you were supposed to
do, idiot. With tickets to the hottest concert of the
summer, you could have put an ad in the paper and
had a *hundred* women lined up—"

"Come on, she appreciated it. She'll remember
it next time—"

"Dork. She used the S word, Stanley. She called you 'sweet.' "

"So?"

" 'Sweet' is female talk for 'loser.' For 'I want to be friends.' For 'I love you—like a brother.' For 'There ain't gonna be a next time, chump.' "

"You are a bitter, bitter man, Charlie. A cynic."

"Oh, yeah? The sweet guys get to sit around and be shoulders to cry on when women like Maggie moan and complain about the sons of bitches they really love, which ain't never, ever gonna be you, pal. 'Sweet' you put in your coffee."

"Charlie—"

"Let me ask you this, Stan my man. What was her girlfriend from out of town's name again?"

"Susan. Uh, no, it was . . . Sharon?"

"Uh-huh. Isn't it real interesting how her best friend's name changed halfway through the conversation, hmm? You've been had, schmuck. Cut so fast you don't even know you're bleeding." He shook his head. "Stanley, Stanley, Stanley."

Stanley's heart hit a reef and went down with all hands. Charlie was right.

"Hey, cheer up, pal. Life isn't all bad. Tell you what. What say, let's hit the streets tonight. Go on a little *luuuvvvv* safari."

"Excuse me?"

"Well, you're gonna take care of those stats, right? Let me make it up to you. I'll take you to the Coco Bongo Club, the newest and the hippest, and where only the crème de la crème need bother to apply."

"Yeah? How do *we* get in?"

"Not to worry, Stanleeto, *I'll* handle it. Leave it to Mr. Cool, I have my—whoa, *baby*!"

Stanley turned to look in the direction of Charlie's openmouthed gaze.

A young woman had just come through the glass-and-brass revolving doors. She had a soggy newspaper over her head and it hadn't done her much good. She was soaked. She paused and tossed the wet paper into the trash can, then tried to straighten her clothes.

She was drop-dead gorgeous. A willowy strawberry blonde with ice-blue eyes and a face that would easily launch a thousand ships. She made Maggie look like an old boot. Both Stanley and Charlie were hypnotized. Stanley felt like a sparrow watching a snake about to eat him. He couldn't have looked away from this vision of beauty if there'd been an earthquake.

Charlie said, "My God. I believe I am losing control."

"Roll your tongue back into your mouth, Charlie."

"I'll let her do it. After she's done with it, I mean."

The woman turned and saw the two men. Smiled at them. The flash of that smile reminded Stanley of the radio station he sometimes caught on the bounce late at night when the conditions had been right when he was a kid: "Hello, America! This is K-A-A-Y in Little Rock, Arkansas, fifty thousand watts of *pure power*!"

Pure power. Amen.

The woman walked toward them. "Excuse me, where can I open a new account?" she asked.

"Here," Charlie said. "Right here. New accounts, that's me. Have a seat. Please."

Stanley turned away, moving toward his own desk five feet away.

Paradise viewed, but paradise lost. Again. He knew how Moses must have felt. The Promised Land, but not for you, sinner . . .

But when he got back to his desk, he turned and saw the vision standing next to it.

Behind her, Charlie stared at them.

If looks could kill, Stanley knew he'd'd've burned a spot on the carpet.

"Uh, uh, what kind of account did you want to open, Miss, uh . . . ?"

"Carlyle. Tina Carlyle." She peeled off her wet blazer and hung it over the back of the chair. It was a sight worth telling one's grandchildren about, Stanley thought. Assuming he ever got lucky enough to *do* anything that might someday result in grandchildren.

She put her shoulder bag on his desk. She sat. Crossed her legs. Damp nylon whispered a siren song to Stanley.

"Interesting tie," she said.

Stanley resisted a sudden urge to rip the tie off and offer it to her.

"Mister . . . ah . . . ?"

Stanley blinked. "Ipkiss. Stanley Ipkiss."

"Pleased to meet you, Stan. Can I call you Stan?"

"You can call me anything you want." There, he thought. That was fairly witty, wasn't it?

She smiled again. Stanley was bathed in the supernal glow. He would have been content to sit there and bask in the gleam for a while.

Days. Weeks. Years.

Aeons . . .

"That pattern kind of looks like one of those ink-blot things," she continued, nodding at his tie.

"Rorschach test?"

"Yeah, that's it. That spot right there, it kind of looks like Lady Godiva riding naked on horseback, doesn't it?"

Stanley swallowed, his mouth suddenly as dry as a boxcar full of white vermouth. What it had always looked like to him was a black blob on a yellow tie, but who was he to argue?

"Uh, yeah, I suppose. . . ."

"Or maybe two lovers. That's the woman on top, right there, sitting up." She reached out and touched his tie with her forefinger.

Stanley stared at her, mesmerized. "My—my mother bought me this tie."

"How interesting she must be. Your mother."

Stanley picked up a pencil from the desk and

carefully shoved it into the pencil sharpener. He smiled, Mr. Cool.

The sharpener made an ugly grinding sound, and when he looked at it, he realized it wasn't a number-two pencil jammed into it but a ballpoint pen.

Black ink dribbled onto the desk.

Oops.

He tossed the dead pen into the garbage can as coolly as possible under the circumstances.

"About that, uh, that account?"

"What kind do you have?" She leaned back in the chair and inhaled deeply. An impressive move as far as he was concerned. My. What wonderful lungs she must have.

"We, uh, have savings, checking, savings and checking combined. CDs, saving and CDs, checking and CDs, savings, checking and CDs, T-bills, electronic banking, whatever you want."

She smiled. "Go on. Tell me about them."

Stanley was willing to sit here and talk to her as long as she would listen. After that kick in the *cojones* from—what was the teller's name? Oh, yes, Maggie. After that, this vision was a welcome surprise indeed. And Charlie glowering in the background made it that much, well, *sweeter*.

"Okay. Let's start with your basic checking account, first."

"Start anywhere you want, Stan. I'm all ears."

That, he knew, wasn't true at *all*.

2

Dorian Tyrel fingered the diamond stud in his right ear as he leaned back in his two-grand Sharper Image massage chair and looked at the big color video monitor. He took a toke from his cigarette and blew smoke at the screen. This was his main office, the operations center at the Coco Bongo, and he had spared no expense in outfitting it. Video games, computers, all the latest gear.

Dorian was not stingy with himself, either. He wore a Matsuda jacket, a tailored blue silk shirt, three-hundred-dollar Hong Kong slacks, and hand-made horsehide Italian penny loafers. Instead of pennies in the slots, he had inserted antique gold coins, Roman coins worth more than the rest of his clothes put together. Which was saying something. If you counted the Rolex, he could sell his outfit and buy himself a new house *and* a new car. Up on the hill in Windwood Development and a Mercedes convertible, easy, *plus* somebody to mow the grass and wash the car. With change left over for the paper boy and doughnuts every morning for a year, too.

The image on the screen was of the vault inside the Edge City First Bank, courtesy of the minicam built into Tina's purse. Three thousand bucks' worth of camera, but it did what it was supposed to do. It was like he was sitting right there in the bank. Could even see the pattern on the dickweed's tie sitting across from Tina.

Freeze had pulled a chair next to Dorian's and was writing notes into his personal secretary computer. The lanky black man with the elaborate red sculpted do mumbled to himself as he worked. He wore cheap off-the-rack clothes: a blue suit and running shoes. White socks. Man was a genius, but he had no taste whatsoever. Give him a bunch of money and he'd probably go out and buy a load of black velvet paintings and polyester.

"So, what do you think?" Dorian said.

"That Perkins/Jennings time lock ain't no sweat, though I don't like them motion detectors."

"They a problem?"

"Sheeitt, man, you talkin' to the *Doc*tah here. You can tell the Swede it ain't no big thing. I can open this turkey like a bottle o' beer."

Dorian leaned forward, picked up a bottle of Yoo-Hoo from his desk, sipped at it.

Behind them, Sweet Eddy and Orlando, playing air hockey, started yammering at each other again.

"Hey, man, you can't do that, that's cheatin'!" Sweet Eddy said.

"Where's it say that, fool?" Orlando came back.

Dorian turned and looked at the two. They had their jackets off, so their hardware was visible. Sweet Eddy wore a .44-mag Desert Eagle in a droopy shoulder rig; Orlando favored an H&K squeeze-cocker.40 in an inside-the-waistband holster. "Hey, you two want to keep it down to a dull roar back there? We tryin' to do some business here."

The two men glanced at Dorian, then went back to glaring at each other. They dropped their voices to stage whispers.

"You cheatin' scum!"

"In your mouth!"

"In my mouth? In your *Momma's* mouth!"

"Don't you be dissin' my Momma, fool!"

"Shut up!" Dorian yelled. "They like children," he said to Freeze. He shook his head sadly and sipped at the Yoo-Hoo again. "Thing is, Doctah, this ain't exactly the Swede's project."

Freeze looked up from his little computer. "Say what?"

Dorian shrugged, put the drink down on his desk. Carefully, so as not to spill it on any of the high-tech electronics.

Freeze said, "Everything that *hap*pens in this

town is the Swede's project, Dorian. You know that."

"Things change."

Freeze looked at him as if he had just turned into a big lizard. Said, "Yeah, things change. Instead of being alive and breathing the nice hot smoggy air, you could get to be pushing up the daisies. Takin' the long dirt nap, you mess with the Swede. That'd be a *change*, all right."

"He's gonna be the one feeding the worms, he messes with me." Dorian reached back and pulled from the wall the poster the Swede had made of himself, the one where he was all pumped up and buffed, flexing in front of the weight machine in his gym. Dorian took a big drag from his cigarette, then used the glowing tip to burn holes through the poster. Right where the Swede's big blue eyes were. He smiled real big as he did it. "Just like that."

"You crazy, Dorian."

"Look, Doctah, with a little money, I can hire some real talent." He nodded at Sweet and Orlando. "Guys with guns *and* brains. Then the Swede, well, let's just say, he is going to *retire*. He's gettin' soft, what it is. He needs to make room for somebody with an edge. I'm going to make it happen. Simple."

"Simple is gone get us killed, that's what you gone do."

"You let me worry about that. You just worry about the bank."

Doctah Freeze shook his head, but he bent back

to his computer. He was a technician, not a thinker. Thinking was Dorian's department. The Swede had been in charge long enough. It was time for new juice. *His* juice.

He took another hit from the cigarette, then leaned forward to stub it out in the carved onyx ashtray. Ashtray had cost him four hundred dollars. He smiled at how it was going to be. He was going to be The Man.

Yeah.

The cab was locked into the downtown Edge City five o'clock traffic grid, barely moving. Horns honked, people cursed. The rain had stopped and given way to smog again. The sun had blasted the sidewalks mostly dry but put the moisture into the air—the humidity had gone almost to a hundred percent, the temperature was well over a hundred, and it came off the pavement in greasy, smelly waves.

Just another day trapped in paradise.

Inside the cab, Charlie and Stanley sat, listening to the driver yell in a language neither of them could identify. The air conditioner wheezed asthmatically and a bad bearing clattered. It was making more noise than coolness. The back of the cab smelled like a combination of beer, pee, and old vomit.

Charlie said, "You tell 'em, Sparky." He looked at Stanley. "I love this guy. Lithuanian, you think? Bulgarian? Transylvanian?"

Stanley stared through the grimy window. Saw a kid on a tricycle pedal past in the same direction they were supposed to be going. Said, "We're going to die and cook in this thing. A four-year-old just outran us. I think I saw a turtle with a broken leg zip past us a minute ago." He didn't like being in the cab. He had a touch of claustrophobia, from when some of the kids at his grammar school had locked him into a trunk backstage at the auditorium and left him there. He been in the trunk for half a day. When the teacher had finally heard him screaming, she'd let him out, only to send him to the principal's office for skipping class. Everybody thought he had gotten into the trunk on his own and nobody wanted to hear otherwise. If he hadn't known it before then, that little incident convinced him there wasn't any justice in the world. He'd had to memorize ten pages of poetry as a punishment, including "Invictus." Boy, had *that* guy been full of it.

"Ah, Stanley, you worry too much. You got to learn to go with the flow."

"Flow? What flow? We're moving at one mile an hour. When we move."

They looked at the sidewalk. An old lady using a walker passed them. He had to get out of here or he really was going to start screaming.

"That's it. I'm gone," Stanley said. He reached for the door handle. The cab lurched forward. Almost caught up the with the old lady. Slowed enough so she started gaining on them again.

Lord, Lord.

"Hey, hold it up, please," Stanley said.

The driver twisted in his seat, revealing a swart, hairy face under a thick, single bar of eyebrow. A face that had way more than its share of nose. A face with at least three gold teeth in it.

A panel in the scratched and filthy bulletproof Lexan slid back and the pitted bore of an old Parkerized .45 appeared in the opening.

Stanley froze. He didn't even blink.

The driver said, "You no hold up me! I keel you very much well! I spatter your guts all the time! I'm your purse nightmare!"

Charlie said, "No! No! Not a holdup! He wants you to stop the cab, that's all! No holdo upo, understando?"

The driver jerked the pistol back through the slot, slid the panel shut. "Ah, I understand very good. Okay, pardon you very much."

Stanley shoved the door open and leaped out. Turned and stared back at Charlie, who slid over and rolled the window down.

Charlie said, "Okay, buddy, so get your exercise. Ten o'clock at the Coco Bongo, remember the directions I gave you. It'll be great. You're gonna love it!"

By the time Stanley got to Ripley's Auto Shop, he was grimy with smog and city dirt, mixed to a scummy paste with his own sweat. He had loosened his tie and undone his top button, but it hadn't helped much. He felt like death, not just warmed over, but baked to a sodden, putrid brown.

Stanley Ipkiss, this is your life.

Bleh.

Ripley's looked more like a graveyard for dead autos than a repair place. Half-dismembered car bodies were everywhere. Leaky tubs of grease, waste oil, and other less identifiable liquid squatted in dark puddles here and there. The smell was beyond words. Dirty sawdust coated the floor. The counter in front was stacked with parts catalogs and fan belts and broken headlamps, all covered in black fingerprints and smears of yellow lube. Somewhere unseen, a mechanic who believed in the use-a-bigger-hammer philosophy of repair whanged something solid—*clang! clang! clang!*—over and over as regular as a metronome.

Nobody else seemed to be around.

Stanley stared at a calendar on the wall. Miss Power Tool for July—July five years ago—looked at the camera in a kind of half turn. She was flawless. Well, except for what was obviously a pair of greasy lip prints on her bare bottom.

There was a bell on the counter, one of those old metal service things, and Stanley tapped it. How anybody could hear it over the racket in back—a power wrench kicked on at the moment he touched the bell—he didn't know. He waited a couple of minutes for the wrench and the hammer to die down, then hit the bell again.

"Hey, anybody home?"

Five more minutes passed.

"Hey!" he yelled. "Anybody back there? Hey!"

A behemoth of a man lumbered into view, wiping his greasy hands on a rag that might have once been red but was now as black as Stanley's mood. "Don't get your panties in a wad. I'm comin'." He wore a work shirt and the name "Sam" was barely visible under the layers of crud. As he passed what looked to be a mortally wounded Oldsmobile, a thin, weasel-faced man popped up from under the raised hood, holding a tangle of wires. He waved the mess at the bigger man. "Hey, Burt, what the hell is this?"

The giant rubbed at his chin with one hand, adding to the grime on his face. "I dunno. About seven hundred bucks, be my guess."

Both men laughed. It was an evil chorus.

Stanley shook his head.

The golem shambled toward him. "Yeah? What is it, bub?"

"Sam?"

"Nah, he died. But the shirt fits." He tapped the name over the pocket. "I'm Burt."

"I'm here to pick up my car. The Civic."

Burt started pawing through a gelid mass of work orders on the counter. "Civic. Civic. Oh, yeah, kind of a snot-green color?"

"It's emerald forest. I brought it in for an oil change, I got that discount coupon in the mail—"

Burt turned his back on Stanley and yelled, "Hey, Irv! What about that snot-green Civic?"

The weasel-faced man popped up into view again and walked toward them, wiping his hands on his own grease-soaked rag, something that only made his hands worse. "You the Civic?"

"Yes, I'm the—is it done yet?"

Irv shook his head. "Well, the thing is, the brake drums are shot and the transmission is practically gone."

"What? All I came in for is an oil change!"

"Lucky you did, pal. You only got fifteen percent left in the front, maybe ten percent in back. One good panic stop and your brakes are kaput! Plus that tranny could drop out at any time. You're driving a death machine, buddy, could go at any minute. Take you, the wife, the kids, two or three innocent bystanders, you know what I mean?"

Stanley stared at him.

"Up to you, if you're ready to die."

Burt smiled. "Yep, you fix it or get buried in it. Up to you. Oh, here's your complimentary comb." He offered Stanley an unwrapped black comb. Two of the teeth were missing and it was coated in what looked to be sixty-weight oil. It—or maybe Burt's hand—smelled as if it had been used to clean out a septic tank.

"So, you wanna fix the snot-green Civic or what?"

"Uh, well, uh . . . yeah, I guess if it needs it—"

Burt dropped the comb onto the counter. "Here. Sign this. Press down hard."

Stanley looked at the curled and greasy form. "There's no price on it."

"Don't worry, we'll put that in later."

"How much will it cost?"

"Hey, do I look like I got a crystal ball, bub? We got to get in there and see how long it takes. This isn't like paint by numbers, you know. We have to be flexible. We'll call you."

"Uh, well, the coupon says if you keep the car more than one day, you provide a loaner."

Burt chuckled. "Yeah, it does, don't it? Hey, Irv, go get the loaner and bring it around front." He looked at Stanley again. "We provide the loaner—a late-model foreign sports car in this case—but you gotta fill it with gas."

A *sports* car? Wow. "Gas? Oh, sure, I can do that."

He had a sudden vision of himself arriving in front of the Coco Bongo Club in a low-slung Italian rocket-on-wheels. Or maybe an Aston-Martin.

Who is that? the women would all wonder.

That? Why, that's Ipkiss. Stanley Ipkiss. With the British Secret Service. He's one of the double-O operatives. Licensed to kill, you know . . .

"And there's a nominal charge for insurance," Burt said, breaking into his fantasy.

"Insurance?"

"Nineteen bucks a day."

"Nineteen dollars a *day*? I can rent a car for that much!"

"If you don't mind walking twenty blocks to the

nearest place to get one. Looks to me like it's gonna rain again." He grinned.

Stanley shook his head. Twenty blocks in this city would cook you or get you mugged. Or both: some places they would mug you and then eat you. He shook his head again. They had him. No way out. The story of his life.

He signed. "I'll take the loaner."

"Thought you would. Sign here, bub. Press down hard. And here, here's another coupon book. We'll call you when the car is ready, probably won't be more than a week or ten days, we don't get too busy." He gave Stanley another smile. "And hey, you have a nice day."

Stanley stood staring after Burt and Irv as they shuffled away. *Dear Lord. What did I do to deserve this?*

3

A pearlescent blue '54 Bentley glided to a stop in front of the Coco Bongo Club. The light drizzle falling on the car gave the paint a brighter sheen under the neon lights over the club's entrance.

An attendant zipped around the car and had the door open in two seconds, smiling at the young Turk behind the wheel. A second attendant arrived with a golf umbrella to shelter the driver as he stepped out.

The driver looked like he was maybe twenty-two years old.

Probably a record producer, Stanley thought. Or a dope dealer.

The next car in line was a fire-engine-red Ferrari and the leggy six-foot-tall blonde who stepped out was a model whose face had appeared on the cover of every woman's slick in the country in the last year. Plus half the magazines in Europe.

A classic two-tone tan-and-burgundy Corniche oozed to a liquid stop behind the Ferrari. A man in an Armani tux and a woman in a plain black evening gown that probably cost as much as Stanley made in six months alighted from the Corniche. Attendants with umbrellas that sprouted like mushrooms scurried to protect the tux and gown.

Must be nice.

Stanley took a deep breath and urged the loaner forward. It went, but reluctantly, sputtering, coughing, dragging itself as though mortally wounded, as though it had a spear thrust through its bowels.

The "sports" car was a fifteen-year-old dead-paint-red-and-Spackle-gray Citroën well into its second hundred thousand miles. Or maybe the third. The muffler was rusted out and it rumbled like a coal miner with silicosis. He kept expecting the car to spit a great glob of phlegm, the way it continually hawked and cleared its throat.

His arrival-at-the-club fantasy had altered somewhat:

Who is that?

That? Why, that's Ipkiss, the loser. You know how much he's paying for that thing he's in? Nineteen *dollars a day*—plus *gas*.

You're kidding. . . .

The Citroën clattered to a stop. The laboring engine gave up the current fight; it uttered a death rattle and a smelly black poot of exhaust, then went silent.

The parking attendant raised his eyebrows so high Stanley thought they might leave his head and fly away into the rainy night.

Stanley smiled at him through the pitted window. More of a pained grimace, actually.

The attendant sauntered over, in no hurry, and reached for the door handle. Tugged on it.

It wouldn't open.

He jerked harder.

The door held fast.

Stanley threw his shoulder against the door. Nothing. He slammed into it again while the attendant pulled with all his might. The door *grinched* with a sound like a flagpole-size nail being pulled from wet wood and sprang open.

The attendant fell down.

Stanley stepped out, dusted the front of his black sport coat. Smiled at the couple in tux and evening gown, who had stopped to stare at his arrival. He patted the roof of the Citroën. "It's a classic, you know. Belonged to Elvis." For his trouble, he got an astonished stare and a palm coated with wet rust and filler.

The umbrellas seemed to have become extinct. The light rain pattered onto Stanley's head.

The attendant slid into the car, winced when a bad spring stuck him in the butt, and tried to restart the car.

No good. He got out, waved two more attendants over. They helped him push it away.

Stanley looked up to see Charlie grinning at him. Charlie was sporting the retro Don Johnson look tonight: unshaven, a white silk sport coat, very wrinkled, a flowered shirt and yellow linen slacks, also wrinkled, with gray leather miniboots.

"Hey, Stanleeto! Whatcha driving there, a Rolls Canardly?"

"A what?"

"You know, rolls down a hill, can hardly roll up the next one?"

He cracked up at his own lame joke. Stanley just stared at him. From a man dressed like an escapee from a circus, he had a lot of room to be laughing. Charlie probably had hair on his palms.

"So this is the great Coco Bongo Club," Stanley managed to say. There must have been three hundred people standing out there in the rain. Some had umbrellas, most did not. Amazing. Then he looked up to see a poster on the wall, a life-size image of a beautiful woman. It took him a second to realize who it was: Tina Carlyle. The woman from the bank.

"Hey, isn't that . . . ?"

"Yep," Charlie said. "The goddess you stole from me."

"I didn't steal anything—"

"Never mind. Looks like she's the singer here. Honeys like that don't have real jobs. Hello? There they are. Maybe two of my future ex-wives! Girls!

Over here!" He waved, and Stanley looked over to see two racy-looking women in halter tops and miniskirts waving back at Charlie. The wet clothes stuck to them like paint. The term *T&A* came to Stanley's mind.

"It's Pebbles and Barbie," he said.

Stanley shook his head. "Pebbles and Barbie? Doesn't it bother you that all the women you know are named after cartoon characters?"

Charlie smirked at him. "At least I *know* some women. How's Betty these days?"

The two young women hurried over to where Charlie and Stanley stood. "Hey, Charlie! We've been out here for, like, you know, hours! They won't let us in. We're like, getting soaked!"

Charlie slid an arm around each woman's waist. "Not to worry girls, I'll have a word with the proper authorities. This is my friend Stanley Ipkiss. Stanley is humongo in the banking biz, you know."

The two women spared Stanley a glance. Took in his black sport coat and dismissed him. What? Was there dandruff on it again? Maybe it was true what they said about black sport jackets, they did seem to pick up everything but women and money. Sure picked up dog hair; look, there was some of it right there. He brushed at it, smiled at the girls.

Charlie dragged the two tittering women away through the damp crowd, working his way toward two Schwarzenegger clones in tight T-shirts and parachute pants behind a red velvet rope under a roof overhang.

Stanley followed.

"Hey, Bobby! Bobby!" Charlie yelled at the nearer hulk. "What's happenin', man? *Qué pasa?*"

Bobby must be deaf, Stanley thought. He didn't turn toward Charlie but moved the velvet rope aside to allow a pasty-faced rock star and a girl who looked to be pushing all of fifteen pass through and into the club.

Charlie smiled at Stanley and the girls. "Just take a second, here." He pointed himself at the other bouncer. "Yo, Nick! Nicky, baby! It's me, Charlie!"

Nick must have had his hearing aid turned off, too. He stared straight ahead.

Stanley shook his head. This was degrading. Standing in the rain, begging for favors. Being ignored by those two steroid jockeys who probably sported IQs equal to their chest size.

Charlie said, "Stanley, how much cash you carrying?"

Stanley blinked. "Huh?"

"Cash, dinero, baksheesh, how much you got on you?"

"Fifty, sixty bucks." What was left of his stereo system after he'd bought the tickets to the Mega-Puke concert. All of the cash he currently owned.

"Gimme."

"Hey, forget it."

"Come on, all I got is plastic, I'll pay you back. Sometimes you have to oil the wheels a little, you

know what I mean?" He nodded at the bodybuilders. "Unless you want to stand out here all night?"

Stanley looked over at Tina's poster. Well, it
would be nice to see her again. And Barbie and Pebbles weren't so bad. He wasn't looking for a conversation with Einstein, was he? He pulled his wallet
out.

Charlie grabbed the wallet and plucked the bills
from it, then tossed it back at him. He elbowed his
way through the throng toward the rope and held
the bills in front of his belt. "Yo, Bobby!"

The bodybuilder's radar pinged and he smiled
at Charlie. Must be able to smell the money. "My
man! Long time no see! Howya doing?"

He unsnapped the rope and got the cash hand-
shake as Charlie stepped through.

Pebbles and Barbie rushed the gap and the
crowd surged after them. Stanley struggled behind,
but the press was like a big wave, too much for him.
He got to the rope as the bodybuilder snapped the
hook back into place.

"Hey! I'm with them! With Charlie!"

Bobby's eyes and ears had glazed over again. He
didn't look at Stanley.

Stanley grabbed the thick velvet cord.

Both Bobby and Nicky pounced on him like
ducks on a june bug. They lifted him clear off the
sidewalk.

"Hey! Leggo!"

"You don't touch the rope," Bobby said.

"Never, ever," Nicky agreed. "You *never* touch the rope."

A tall and sharply dressed man with a diamond-stud earring stepped out of the club and looked at the bodybuilders where they held Stanley up like a rag doll. "Trouble?"

"No, sir, Mr. Tyrel. This guy was just leaving."

"Good."

Bobby and Nicky grinned at each other. "On three, okay?" Bobby said.

"One . . . two . . . *three!*"

They tossed Stanley into the crowd as if he were no heavier than a pillow. The crowd parted like the Red Sea under Moses' staff and Stanley hit the damp pavement on his butt.

"Oof!"

He stood, brushed his pants off, and glared back at the bodybuilders. Great. Just great!

He took a few steps toward the street, got to the curb. He ought to go back and tell those two idiots what he thought of them. He ought to spit in their eyes, that's what he ought to do. But he knew he wouldn't. It wasn't in him to do that kind of thing, to stand up to people. He *wanted* to, but what he probably would do would be go somewhere and cry—

A stretch limo whipped past. The tires found a deep puddle of muddy rainwater in a pothole and splashed nearly all of it onto Stanley, where he stood dreaming his revenge fantasy. It drenched him.

As he stood there dripping wet, feeling about as low as he'd felt in his life, and that was *saying* something, the limo pulled to a stop fifteen feet past him. The door opened and a woman in a red evening gown stepped out under the umbrella the chauffeur held for her.

Tina Carlyle.

Oh, no. The last person on Earth he wanted to see right now.

Stanley stared. Maybe she wouldn't see him. Maybe the sidewalk would open up and swallow him—

No such luck. The woman of his dreams turned and looked right at him.

Well. At least she wouldn't know who he was—

"Mr. Ipkiss? Stan?"

Take me, Lord. Please. Send a lightning bolt to fry me. Please.

Through some miracle, the carhops had managed to get the Citroën started. It arrived now, sputtering and farting, and stopped in front of Stanley.

Tina looked at the car, then back at him.

"Uh, this is just a loaner. My car's in the shop. Being, uh, you know, prepared for the big race."

"Race?"

"Yeah, the uh, uh, Tallahassee . . . huh, Three Thousand. I've won it, like four years in a row . . . consecutively, that is."

"Really. How nice."

"Yeah, my cars have caught on fire, like . . . eight times. You, uh, get used to it."

The car attendant stepped around and stood in front of Stanley. "Your . . . car, sir."

Stanley reached into his pocket, came up empty. He'd given all his money to Charlie. Jeez.

"Well, nice to see you again, Stan. Good luck in the race." She turned and was escorted toward the door. The wet crowd began to applaud as she passed.

Stanley looked at the Citroën. Why did all the gods hate him so much? What had he done to deserve this?

"See you," he said to the attendant.

"Christ, I hope not. I'm gonna have to go visit a proctologist as it is, pal."

Stanley climbed into the moaning car and drove off. Maybe if he got real lucky, a Mack truck would hit him on the way home.

As he pulled away from the club, the car wheezing as if it were about to give up the ghost again, he looked into the rearview mirror. All the glitter and expensive shine back there as the crowd worked its way toward the entrance, that was what he wanted. To rub shoulders—and other parts of himself—with the rich and famous. Was that so wrong? To be somebody of worth, among other people of worth?

It wasn't like he wanted to hurt anybody or step on them to get to the top. He was willing to work for it, work hard as need be, but somehow the opportunity never seemed to open up for him. He used to dream of saving the mayor's life or rescuing people from bandits or like that. They would all be so grateful to him, the rewards—and more important—the *admiration* would shower on him. So he would get his chance to shine. He could do it, he knew he could, if only he had a chance, that's all he wanted. He didn't need it handed to him on a silver platter, he just needed a shot.

Given the way his life had gone so far, a shot was what he was likely to get. A fast bullet in the head. Or maybe a big meteor would fall out of the rainy sky and land on him.

The way he felt right now, either would be an improvement.

He sighed, and drove.

4

The ailing Citroën wheezed its way up the slight incline leading to the old Burnside Bridge over the Tahoochie River. The engine sputtered, the muffler popped, and Stanley hunched over the wheel, urging the car along—as if leaning forward would help.

"Come on, baby, you can do it. It's just a little old bridge. I know how you feel, you're tired of it all, but we're two of a kind, you and me. I *know* you can do it."

Fortunately, traffic was light. That way, when the engine had a stroke and expired almost at the top of the short rise, nobody plowed into the Citroën's rear end as it rolled to a stop. It did not go gently into that good night. With the motor dead, he could hear the ungreased bearings in the tires squeaking, the shocks groaning and pissing away what little fluid they had left.

So much for his nineteen-dollar-a-day *sports* car. Well, *fine!*

Here he was, on a bridge, sitting in something that made his old snot-green Civic look like a new Lexus.

He tried the key several times, but the starter just ground away uselessly until the battery went dead.

RRRNNNN-uh-uh-uh . . . uh . . .

He banged his shoulder against the door until God's claw hammer pulling another giant nail from the condemned House of Doom sounded and allowed the door to open. He got out and stared at the car.

A van full of teenagers went past. They offered helpful solutions at the tops of their lungs, along with commentary on his manhood, his incestuous relationship with his mother, and the composition of his cranium. They added big dollops of laughter to the obscene mix, then sped away.

Normally, he liked children. This particular batch ought to be horsewhipped, then taken out and shot. Stanley walked around to the front of the car. Enraged, he kicked the bumper.

The car responded by dropping the bumper, very nearly on his foot.

He leaped back.

The front axle snapped. The Citroën sagged in the middle. The front tires splayed, the hubcaps fell off. As did, a moment later, the driver's door. It was kind of like one of those time-lapse movies of ants eating a mouse.

He stared at the dead car. If he saw this in a movie, he wouldn't believe it. How could one man's luck be so rotten?

Perfect. Just perfect!

Stanley walked to the railing and stared down at the muddy Tahoochie below him. It gurgled past with bayoulike slowness. The odor of sewage was strong, even high above the water. He noticed that one of the buttons on his coat sleeves was loose. He picked at it. It came off in his fingers. He sighed and tossed it over the side of the bridge. It vanished in the dark. Well. At least it had stopped raining.

Sometimes you had to really look hard for that silver lining.

Like maybe, since he was on a bridge and all, he should just jump.

It was a solution to all his problems and he had considered it or variations of it several times over the years. Jumping from a building or a bridge didn't really appeal—what if by some freak accident you survived the leap? Then you'd really be in great shape, wouldn't you? Miserable *and* crippled. And he didn't have a gun or poison. The one time he'd gone to a doctor to try to get sleeping pills for his insomnia, the guy had given him Benadryl to help him get drowsy. An overdose of that would probably dry his eyeballs and tongue out, but he wasn't sure it would kill him.

He'd considered hanging himself. Rope was cheap, he could rig up something in his apartment, and the idea that the dreaded Mrs. Peenman might be the one to find the week-old corpse and be greatly disturbed by it brought with it a small but warm glow. Then again, given how the old dragon was, what was more likely to happen would be that she'd see his dangling body and rejoice—she could raise the price on his rent-controlled apartment. Probably clean out his tapes and wallet before she called the cops, too. The idea of her pawing through his stuff after he was dead was revolting. He was pretty sure she would sneak in while he was gone and do it while he was alive, except for Milo.

Had to look for a silver lining even in suicide, too—

Then he saw the body.

"My God!"

There was a *body* snagged on some branches next to the bank, eddying in the current.

"Hey! You in the water! Are you okay?"

Stanley, what kind of moron are you? You think somebody is out for a late-night swim in all their clothes in the Tahoochie? That river water is so vile you could use it to clean the chrome on your car—if you *had* a car. Word was, it would eat the dead gray paint off the side of a battleship.

Stanley ran for the end of the bridge.

He slid and fell down the slope a couple of times on his way to the river's edge. He ducked under an old ladder that leaned against a bridge piling, stepped on a piece of mirror in the muck and shattered it, and almost tripped on a black cat, but got to the river in time to see the body break loose from the branches and swirl away.

Stanley squished through the knee-deep mud, lunged into the river, and waded out in waist-high water, caught the body—

Which came apart in his hands.

It wasn't a body. It was a *garbage* bag, an old coat, and a glob of seaweed all wound together by the roiling water.

Hello? What's this?

The ersatz figure's "head" came apart when he grabbed at it, but what he wound up with was what looked like a wooden mask.

He sloshed back ashore, clutching the mask. On land again, he examined the thing as best he could under the city glow. A sudden break in the clouds allowed the full moon to shine through, and he got a better look at it. Wood, with some kind of arcane symbols carved into it, a strange, leering grin, and big and eerie empty eyeholes. Covered with slime, grease, goo, and God knew what else.

He felt a sudden chill.

Well. Summer night or not, he *was* all wet and muddy.

He raised the mask and held it closer to his face. It seemed to shimmer in the moonlight, almost as if it were lit from within. . . .

A frog croaked behind him and he jumped. "Jeez!"

Suddenly a spotlight splashed over him. Stanley blinked and looked up.

A police car was parked on the bridge behind the dead Citroën. A cop stood next to it with the spot, looking down at Stanley. "Hey, pal, this your heap?"

"Uh, yeah. It's a rental."

"And whaddaya doing down there?"

Stanley couldn't think of a reasonable answer. So he held the mask up. "I, uh, dropped my mask. Had to come down and get it."

Lame, Stanley. Lame, lame, lame.

Dorian smiled at Tina as he watched her collect the sheet music from the piano. He held up his drink in a silent toast as she walked over to where he sat on his stool at the bar.

Doctah Freeze, Sweet Eddy, and Orlando sat at the other end of the bar, playing with a cup of dice.

"How did I do, baby?" Tina said as she reached for the bottle of Chivas on the bar and poured herself a drink.

"The best show was the one you did at the bank."

She took a slug of the scotch and glared at him. "I'm not doing that kind of work anymore, Dorian. I'm a singer now."

"Yeah, I recall your red-hot career before I found you."

"Look, don't push me. I might just take that walk I've been telling you about."

He put his arm around her shoulder and pulled her closer to him. "Yeah? And who's gonna kiss you like old Dorian, huh? Who's got the magic in his mouth? Huh? Who?"

She cracked a smile.

"That's what I thought," he said.

He leaned forward and brought his lips toward hers. She raised a finger and touched them. "Not in front of the help," she said. She nodded at the boys.

Dorian laughed.

She turned and walked out.

"She cracks me up, she does," he said. "She kills me."

Doctah Freeze idled over toward him, sipping at his drink. "She might do that someday, you ax me. She not a woman you want to fool around with."

"Ah, lighten up, Doctah. Here's to the Edge City First Bank, who's taking care of all our money for us."

He raised his glass.

Freeze nodded. "I can drink to that."

They did.

Stanley stood on the sidewalk in front of his brownstone and watched the cop car pull away. It had not been a good day. But at last he was home safe. He started for the entrance.

The rusty fire escape in the alley rattled. Something thudded against the ground.

Six or seven young men emerged from the dark alley. They wore artfully slashed pants, leather vests or sleeveless T-shirts, or were bare-chested. A couple of them without shirts had nipple rings glittering under the streetlight, and the number of holes from assorted piercings in ears, nostrils, lips, and other places unseen might well fill the Albert Hall. Their hair was dyed in phosphorescent pink, green, blue, or all three. All of them had somewhere on their clothing or tattooed on their bodies a grinning skull.

Here were the Death Heads, one of the local street gangs.

Well, well, well. What a *perfect* way to end a *perfect* day.

Stanley was almost too tired to care.

"Got out of a cop car," the first Death Head to get close said. "You some kind of undercover *po*-leeceman? Got a nine hidden under your rags? One of them nice German SIGs?" Maybe he was the leader. He had blue hair, cropped to about peach-fuzz length. "I like that German iron."

Stanley looked down at his muddy and still-soaked clothes. "Yeah, that's me, Dirty Harry. You want to make my day? You want to play 'Misty' for me?"

The Death Heads looked at each other. Not a group he was going to bluff for long. What was the point?

He sighed. "Look, guys, I don't have any money, no car, no woman. All I got is this." He held the wooden mask up. "And you are welcome to it." He tossed the mask toward the group. Blue Fuzz fumbled with it, dropped it, picked it up, and looked at it. Wrinkled his nose in disgust. "What, you been

shoveling shit with this thing? It's all slimy, man."
He tossed it back to Stanley, wiped his hands on his
grimy pants. "Keep it." He wiped his hands on his
slashed jeans again, looked at them, then stepped to
within a couple of feet of Stanley. "You got us all
wrong, pal. We don't want any trouble, do we,
boys?"

The other Death Heads nodded and made
agreement walla:

"No, man."

" 'Course not."

"Un-uh. No trouble."

"All I want to know is, do you have the time?"

Stanley stared at Blue Fuzz for a second, then
managed a small smile. Despite himself, he felt a
great sense of relief. "Oh. Yeah, I guess so." He
pulled back his sodden sleeve to look at his watch.
Fortunately it was waterproof. His high-school
graduation present.

Blue Fuzz produced a butterfly knife. He did a
fast twirl with it, grabbed Stanley's wrist, and
neatly slid the blade under the alligator watchband.
Sliced the tough leather easily and caught the watch
as it sprang off Stanley's wrist.

Stanley was too stunned to move.

"My. Look at that!" Blue Fuzz said. "It's way,
way past midnight. You better get home before you
turn into a pumpkin'!" He laughed, a sound like
somebody with a bad cold blowing his nose, then
lunged forward and shoved Stanley.

The other thugs had moved in to form a circle

around him. Stanley fell, but was caught and thrown back at Blue Fuzz. Fuzz stepped aside like a matador, and Stanley stumbled across the circle and was grabbed by a beefy goon with a pink Mohawk. Pink Mohawk hurled Stanley back into the circle.

Everybody but Stanley laughed.

Stanley made two more circuits before he saw his chance. As he got shoved toward a Death Head with a safety pin through his lower lip, he ducked under Pin Lip's outstretched arms and scooted for the door.

The Death Heads laughed and let him go. He fumbled with the key, got the door open, slammed it behind him.

Man!

Now he was safe!

His wet shoes squeaked but he moved as quietly as he could otherwise. He was almost to his apartment, passing Mrs. Peenman's next to his, when the manager's door flew open and the dreaded apparition stood there.

If you took a dragon and shrank it to human size, then gave it hair curlers and the world's ugliest bathrobe, you'd have Mrs. Peenman. Every time she spoke, Stanley fully expected flames to spew from her maw and roast him.

"Ipkiss! Do you know what time it is?"

He glanced reflexively at his now empty wrist. "Uh, actually, no."

"It is three o'clock in the morning! First you wake up the entire building laughing on the doorstep with your hoodlum friends—I could hear you all the way up here on the seventh floor! Then you stomp through the building and—" She stopped and stared at the carpet. "My rug! You are tracking filth all over my rug! This is going to come out of your deposit, Ipkiss!"

Sometimes when he was really tired, he got funny. "Isn't little Jackie Paper waiting for you down at the sailing ship, Mrs. Peenman?"

"What?"

"Nothing. May I go now?"

In answer, she stepped back into her room and slammed the door.

Stanley raised his hands like claws, hunched over, and mimicked a monster's face. "Sanctuary!" he said. Then he turned and headed for his room.

Milo met him at the door, tail wagging, bouncing up and down as if he had springs instead of a mutt terrier's stubby legs.

"Hey, Milo. How are you doing?"

The little dog ran around in a tight circle. He got so excited he went into a coughing spasm, gagging and wheezing.

"Easy, boy, easy. You want me to get the inhaler?"

But the dog calmed down and followed him through the tiny kitchenette into the bedroom. He needed a break, Stanley decided. He stripped off his wet clothes, went into the bathroom, and used a damp washcloth to clean some of the crud off, put on his old pajamas. He went to the tape collection, small but neatly arranged. All his classic cartoons, mostly Tex Avery stuff from the forties. He selected one and popped it into the VCR.

Milo came up behind him, holding the Frisbee in his mouth.

"Aw, come on, Milo, not tonight. I'm beat."

The dog whined.

"All right, all right. Just once." He took the Frisbee and tossed it.

Milo rocketed across the bedroom and into the hall, leaped . . .

Caught the Frisbee perfectly. Brought it proudly back and dropped it at Stanley's bare feet. "Good boy. Now, you need to rest. C'mere, watch the cartoon with me."

Milo hopped up onto the bed and into Stanley's lap.

A bad guy onscreen chased a cartoon dog around in circles. They got to going so fast they became a tornadolike blur. The dog stepped out of the blur, whipped a stick of dynamite from out of nowhere, and lit it. Stepped back into the blur. The scene slowed down. The dog shoved the dynamite into the bad guy's pants. The dog put its paws in its ears and closed its eyes. The bad guy did a take. Said, "Yipe," in a tiny voice. The dynamite went off in a flash of gold and red and yellow. The dog stood to one side, opened one eye, looked at the bad guy, who had turned black. A beat, then the bad guy crumbled to dust. With appropriate sound effects.

Milo yipped and Stanley smiled.

There came a pounding on the wall next to the bed. The framed animation cels on the wall rattled. "Turn that damned thing down!"

Again, the dreaded Mrs. Peenman.

Stanley sighed. He used the remote to pop the tape. A quieter talk show was on under the VCR. Looked like Larry King.

Stanley went back into the bathroom. Put paste on his toothbrush and began to brush his teeth.

The guy being interviewed said, "That's true, Larry. We all wear masks. We repress the id—our darkest desires—and hide behind a socially acceptable facade. Instead of smashing the boss's face in when he yells at us, we smile and nod. Instead of screaming at our nasty landlord, we hold our tongues. This is how we cope with the frustrations of our day-to-day lives, by denying the fight-or-flight hardwiring of a million years and pretending we don't feel the rage. We call this being civilized."

Stanley spat foam. Rinsed his out with a handful of tap water. Grimaced at the metal taste of it. "You got that right, pal," he said to the speaker on the TV. Sometimes he had a fantasy of putting Mrs. Peenman into a room and pumping all the air out. Watching her turn blue through a window, waving bye-bye as she clawed at the glass. Not that he would ever actually *do* it, hurt somebody, but there was no harm in imagining it, was there?

Stanley moved back into the bedroom as the show wrapped up. There was a shot of a book on-screen: *The Masks We Wear*, by Dr. Arthur Neuman.

Stanley hit the power-off button on the remote. Looked at Milo, who was lying on the end of the bed. "I met this beautiful woman today, Milo. A singer. She wanted to take me to Hawaii with her, you know, her treat, but I said I couldn't make it. Too busy being miserable at the bank. Broke her heart, but what can you do? I hate it when they throw themselves at me like that. Too bad. She was gorgeous."

Milo didn't appear to be listening. Instead, he was sniffing at the mask. Suddenly he whined and backed away.

"What's the matter, boy? Something stink on that thing? Here, let me clean it up a little."

He took the mask into the bathroom and rinsed it under the tap. Surprisingly, the crud on it sloughed off easily, as if the mask were made of Teflon or something, and revealed a smooth, finely grained wood. With the muck off of it, the thing looked a lot better than he expected. Hey. Maybe this was like some kind of tribal mask, an antique. Might be worth something.

Yeah? How'd it wind up in the river, then?

Who knows? Maybe somebody stole it and got panicky, threw it away. He held it up. The inside was smooth and clean now. He raised it in front of his face, looked through the eyeholes at the mirror. Interesting.

He pressed it against his face—

5

It was a strange—no—an eerie feeling, like nothing he had ever experienced. The mask expanded, stretched, and snapped over Stanley's head like vacuum shrink wrap. He heard a piercing laugh, something right out of an old radio drama, but three octaves higher. His body temperature went up at least ten degrees. He felt as if he were an overfilled balloon, as if he might puff right up and explode.

Whoa!

Stanley jerked the mask off. It made a noise like an agitated champagne bottle being uncorked.

No way!

He stared at the wooden mask, then at the mirror. Man. He was so tired he was hallucinating. Of course, it *was* almost four A.M. and he'd had a long, ugly, nasty day. And it had been a while since he'd pulled an all-nighter, way back in college. He'd never done psychedelic drugs, but he imagined in that moment he knew what they must feel like.

It was just a piece of carved wood, that was all. He shook his head. Looked at Milo and said, "I thought for a moment there I'd slipped a gear, puppy dog."

Milo looked at him. If a dog's face could show worry, his did.

"But it was just my imagination. Guess I better get some sleep." He started to turn away from the mirror. "But just to prove to myself I'm not nut-so . . ." He pressed the mask against his face and looked at the mirror. "See? No problem."

Milo whined. Stanley turned and saw the dog dive under the bed.

Then things got very strange indeed.

Tendrils of wood shot out of the edges of the mask and wrapped themselves around his head like tentacles. He grabbed at his head and then suddenly, inexplicably, he began to spin. Like a top. Slowly at first, then faster.

In a second, he was twirling like that whirling dervish in the cartoon. He became a whirlwind. Oddly enough, however, he could see himself in the mirror—as if he were standing still and yet rotating with tornadolike speed simultaneously.

The twister spun from the bathroom and into the bedroom.

Milo barked from under the bed.

"Hellllllpppmmeeeee!"

Panicked, Stanley reached for the bedpost, grabbed it.

The spinning stopped, cold.

He took a couple of deep breaths. He looked down, saw a smoking trail burned in the carpet.

He lurched back into the bathroom and looked at the mirror.

The mirror revealed an apparition that made his dragon landlord look like Miss America. His head was green, bald, bug-eyed, and had a rictus that revealed tombstone-shaped teeth three times normal size under a boney, beaky nose.

His pajamas had metamorphosed into a forties zoot suit, big shoulders, long coat, baggy pants, in a distorted version of the paisley they had been.

But, you know, all things considered, he didn't look so bad. In fact, he looked downright charming. He had a certain devil-may-care kind of, well, go ahead and say it, *handsomeness*. In a green sort of way.

Beauty was in the eye of the beholder, after all, wasn't it?

"S-s-s-nazzzzzy, Stan, baby!"

He pulled his bow tie a foot from his neck and let it go. It snapped back with a cartoon *boing!* sound effect, spun like a propeller, then stopped exactly in place.

He turned to his left, to his right, admiring his new profile. If this was a dream—and it had to be, didn't it?—it was very interesting. Might as well go along with it, hey? What could it hurt?

Had he been *tired* a minute ago? C'mon! He
wasn't tired! He felt like a million bucks! Ten million! He wasn't dullhead Stanley anymore, by
cracky, he was The Mask! He could dance all night!
Leap tall buildings. Look up in the sky, it's a bird,
it's a plane, it's . . .

Or not. Anyway, hey, he had to get out of here
and *party*!

"P-A-R-T-Why . . . Because I gotta, that's why!
Twenty-three skiddoo!"

He headed for the door. He'd never felt so good
in his life. No way he was going to look this gift-
horse dream in the mouth.

Out in the hall, he sneaked past the apartment
of the old bat next door, tiptoeing with exaggerated
care. A floorboard creaked.

The Mask held his finger to his lips. "Shhh!"

Suddenly an old-style windup alarm clock the
size of a bowling ball jumped out of his pocket,
bounced on the floor a couple of times, and com-
menced to ringing like crazy.

Where'd that come from?

He leaped at the clock, which dodged his grasp,
hopping hither and yon.

"C'mere!"

The clock thought otherwise. It scooted on its
little legs, ringing to beat the band.

Better do something here. Gonna wake the dead.
Or worse, Mrs. Peenman, the living dead . . .

He produced from his jacket pocket a full-sized
brass-bound wooden stake hammer and swung it at

the fleeing clock. Missed, but put a crater the size of a manhole cover in the floor.

Hey, this *was* fun!

Bam! Thump! Whack!

The clock dodged, but too slow. He caught it a good shot and it cracked—but it kept moving and the bell kept gonging.

"Okay, clocko. You had your chance. Now it's no more Mr. Nice Guy!"

He couldn't *remember* when he'd had so much fun.

He chased the remains of the clock up and down the hall, whacking at it with the sledgehammer. Springs *sproinged*, glass *tinkled*, gear wheels bounced and rolled on the carpet. Wheee!

Where exactly had this hammer come from, anyway?

Oh, well. Who cared?

The clock was getting tired. Running down, maybe? It stopped in front of the door next to Stanley's. Took deep breaths, wheezing. The alarm petered out.

The Mask giggled. "I have you now!" he said in his best deep voice. He raised the hammer. Gonna drive you into the floor like a circus-tent peg, sonny! *Hasta la vista.* You won't be back. The windup and—

The apartment door he was in front of slammed open.

Mrs. Peenman, her hair bound in curlers, stood there, ugly enough to scare the pee out of Medusa.

She got a load of The Mask and screamed.

He got a load of her and screamed back.

Her door slammed.

The Mask looked at the cowering clock. "Thought she'd save you, eh? Say your prayers, clock!"

The door slammed open again. Mrs. Peenman.

With a double-barreled shotgun pointed right at him.

The Mask's eyes bugged out on stalks and his mouth went as wide as a tuba. Hey, nice trick! He said, "Take it easy, lady. I'm just, uh, killin' a little time here."

He thought that was so funny he leaped into the air, hit the ceiling, and began to bounce around the hall like a Super Ball on speed.

No two ways about it, this was sommmme fun!

Mrs. Peenman let go the first barrel. Missed The Mask, blew a fist-sized hole in the wall across the hall.

"You'll never take me alive!"

She fired the other barrel, broke the gun open, and ejected the empty shells, reloaded from her bed-robe pocket.

The Mask bounced past her. Somehow was able to stop right in front of her, still as a photograph. He waggled his eyebrows. "Are we having fun yet?"

She brought the shotgun up and fired both barrels.

The Mask shot down the hall like an arrow, hit the window over the fire escape, crashed through, and sailed into the night air.

Seven stories up.

As he dropped he did the classic falling yodel:

"*Waaah*hhoohoohoohooooo!"

He hit the street in a perfect belly flop and pancaked. Looked as if he'd been run over by a steamroller. Thin as a sheet of paper.

Didn't hurt a bit.

Was this a great dream, or what?

Then, one hand peeled itself loose from the macadam and grabbed the zoot suit's collar. Picked the flattened body up and snapped it like somebody shaking out a towel. There came a *pop!* and The Mask expanded back into full thickness.

Saaay. This was *very* interesting. He was a man of hidden talents. He'd always known that, it was just hard to get them out where they could be admired.

He looked up at the shattered window and yelled, "Better watch that first step, it's a doozy!"

A new El Dorado came around the corner. The driver saw The Mask standing in the middle of the street and slammed on his brakes. He skidded to a stop inches away. Then, this being Edge City, he leaned on his horn.

Edge City folk made New Yorkers look like saints.

The Mask grabbed his ears. Well, where they would be if he *had* ears. Glared at the fat man driving the Cad. "Oh, yeah? See how you like it, pal." He produced a giant bulb horn from under his jacket and pointed it at the Cad. Squeezed the over-sized rubber bulb.

AAAOOOOGGGAAHHHH!

The Cad's windows exploded outward. The headlight blew in. The chrome strips peeled right off the sides and curled up like carrot shavings.

Inside, the driver's hair stood up as if he'd laid hands on a big electrostatic generator.

The Mask tossed the horn over his shoulder. "Have a nice day!"

He turned and boogied away.

As he passed the alley next to the apartment building, a voice from the darkness said, "Hey, mister. You got the time?"

The Mask grinned. Well, well. What do you know. It was Blue Fuzz and the old gang.

He turned around. Slowly.

They saw his face and went pale.

"Jee-zus!" Pink Mohawk said.

"*Madre de Dios!*" Pin Lip said.

"Time? Time, you said? As a matter of fact, why, yes, I do."

The Mask pulled a grandfather clock from his pocket—this was a *great* suit!—and set it on the sidewalk. Looked at it, inclined his head to the left, then the right. "Hmm, wouldja look at that. It's two seconds before I honk your nose and give you a world-class wedgie!"

Blue Fuzz looked puzzled.

The clock gonged like Big Ben.

The Mask jumped, grabbed Blue Fuzz's nose,

and squeezed it. It honked like a cartoon horn. Then he reached down into Fuzz's pants and pulled. Fuzz's jockey shorts came up all the way over Fuzz's head.

Blue Fuzz wheezed a tiny noise. Said, "Ah!"

The Mask grinned wider. "Happy trails, boys!" His legs churned for a second like tires burning rubber, then he caught traction and zipped away and around the nearest corner. Behind him, he could hear the Death Heads as if they were still standing next to him. Super hearing. But of course.

Blue Fuzz tugged his underwear down to his neck. "Get him!"

The others pulled chains, nunchaku, and knives and started after The Mask.

By the time they rounded the corner, The Mask was ready. He was dressed as a carnival barker. Calliope music blared a midway come-on and multicolored lights flashed from nowhere.

The Death Heads skidded to a collective stop.

"Step right up, folks, and see the Wonder of the Ages! The internationally famous Great Maskito— that's a joke, son—the world's foremost magician! Miracles from a hat, wonders as you watch!"

He spun, blurred, and came out of the twirl—

"And now, for my next trick . . ."

Long pink and blue balloons appeared in The Mask's hands. He twisted them together in a frenzy of squeaks and knots and, in a second, had an elaborate balloon sculpture. "Voilà! A giraffe!"

He handed it to Pink Mohawk, who grinned at it like a four-year-old. "Wow," Mohawk said. "Cool."

A true son of Joe Camel, this one.

More balloons appeared and The Mask's hands moved so fast they were a colorful blur. Squeaks, a *pop!* "Oops. Careful! Even the Great Maskito has his off days, you know." A beat later he held a perfect French poodle.

Not bad, not bad, if he did say so himself. He tendered the poodle to Pin Lip.

Blue Fuzz was obviously impressed but beginning to get pissed.

The Mask said, "Ah, now, don't worry, the next one is for you."

Pink and blue skinny balloons appeared and blurred. . . .

"Check *this* out," The Mask said.

He held a Thompson submachine gun. A real one. He pulled the arming bolt back, pointed it at the road in front of the Death Heads, and started shooting.

Jacketed .45 bullets *spanged* and chipped the pavement, ricochets flew every which way, the *rata-tatatat!* and smoke filled the air. "I looove the smell of gunpowder in the morning!"

Death Heads seeking to avoid becoming their name in truth went every which way.

The gun clicked.

"Empty. Oh, well." He tossed the tommy gun over his shoulder. It turned back into balloons and floated away.

The Death Heads cowered under trash cans and behind Dumpsters.

Stanley walked to where Blue Fuzz tried to hide behind an ash bin. "Saaay, friend, do you have the time?"

The Mask reached into Fuzz's pocket and came out with a fistful of watches. Selected one—Stanley's—and dropped the others. Slapped the watch onto his wrist, then turned and walked away, whistling the theme from *The High and the Mighty*.

As he walked The Mask shook his head. This was pretty incredible stuff here. He never knew he had this much juice in him. Why, he *could* be a superhero. He could fight crime, work for world peace, do good deeds. Find a spot, set his lever, and move the world!

Hmm. But these clowns reminded him of something. First, there were a few things he needed to take care of on a *personal* level.

He knew just where he was going to start, too.

There was a single light burning inside Ripley's Auto Shop as The Mask sauntered toward the front door. He heard Burt and Irv inside and, when he peeped through the peephole that magically appeared in the door, saw they were playing cards. Half-eaten chili dogs and empty beer cans littered the table. Tsk, tsk. Messy mechanics.

Burt said to Irv, "Here, pull my finger."

"I *might*. Forget it."

"C'mon. We're talking world class here. Pull it."

Irv reached for Burt's finger. Pulled it.

Timing was all. The Mask kicked the front door and it exploded into little bits.

"Wow, you're weren't kiddin' about it being world class," Irv said.

The two mechanics looked at the shattered door.

Timing. The Mask stepped into the doorway. Put his hands on his hips like a comic book hero.

"Who's there?" Burt asked.

"It is I."

"Who the hell is I? Whaddya want?"

"I'm like the government. I'm here to help you."

Burt and Irv got a good look at The Mask.

Burt let go a poot composed of partially digested chili dog.

"Hmm," The Mask said. "Sounds like a little exhaust problem to me."

He whirled, reached for a pair of mufflers from racks on the wall, pulled them down, and twirled them like six-guns. Snapped them to a halt.

"Maestro?"

"Better fix that leak before it gets serious," The Mask said.

He started toward them.

Burt and Irv screamed. The Mask produced a few SFX to harmonize with their yells. A nice aah-ooga, some whizz-bangs, chirping birds, a fog horn, and here we go. . . .

They tried to run, but they didn't get far.

6

The morning sun came through the gap in the blinds and poked at Stanley's face almost like a hot finger. He pried his eyes open. Gah. How awful. What time was it, anyway? It shouldn't be light yet—

Abruptly he sat up. Grabbed his face.

Normal.

Well. Normal for him, anyway. Needed a shave, bleary eyes, and his mouth tasted like the stained toilet bowl looked, but definitely his own face.

What a weird dream he'd had. He looked at the mask. It was on the top of the TV. Really weird. He couldn't say it felt real—no way—but it had sure been *vivid*; a potent nightmare, although parts of it had been kinda heartwarming. Maybe he'd better ease up on the cartoons. Fantasy was okay, but he didn't want to wind up living in a condo between

Mr. Toad's Wild Ride and Sleeping Beauty's Castle, now, did he?

He rubbed at his beard. He looked at the alarm clock. He'd forgotten to set it.

The clock said he had three minutes to get to work on time.

Jeez!

He put the dream on the back burner as he hopped from the bed and started for the bathroom. He needed to pee, he needed to shave and shower, he'd have to take the damned bus, no way he was going to make it to the bank in less than forty-five minutes. If he were lucky, he might be able to sneak in before Mr. Dickey arrived. Being the owner's son and in charge meant that he never got to work before nine-thirty. Well, almost never. Be Stanley's luck he'd decide to go in early just this once.

Came a knock on the door.

Stanley approached the door carefully. Milo peered from under the bed, but made no move to bark or look fierce for an intruder. Great watchdog he was. He'd lie there and prop the door open for a burglar. Or have an asthma attack and wheeze on the crook's shoes. Well. It wasn't his fault.

"Yeah, who is it?"

"Edge City police."

Stanley swallowed. Like seeing a cop in your rearview, you felt guilty even though you hadn't done anything. He opened the door.

"Police? What can I do for you?"

The cop had a houndlike quality to him, a cheap

suit and brown shoes. He looked as if he'd seen it all twenty years ago and was tired of seeing it over and over again. He looked at a small notebook he held.

"You Stanley Ipkiss?" He looked up from the notebook and stared at Stanley's pajamas.

"That's right."

"I'm Lieutenant Kellaway, Central Precinct. Could you tell me what you know about the disturbance last night, Mr. Ipkiss?"

"Disturbance?"

"Yeah, a prowler. Broke in and attacked the landlord."

"Mrs. Peenman? She was attacked?" What, had some lunatic so far gone he wouldn't run in terror at the first sight of Mrs. Peenman escaped from the asylum?

"She's okay, she scared him off."

"I, uh, I didn't hear anything."

"You didn't *hear* it? The woman next door let loose four rounds of twelve-gauge double-ought buckshot five feet from your door. You sleep with with earplugs? Your head in the freezer?"

Stanley leaned forward a little and looked into the hall.

There were holes in the wall across the way. Craters in the floor. The remains of a giant alarm clock scattered on the carpet.

"Mr. Ipkiss?"

"I, uh, I have an inner-ear problem, Lieutenant." As if to demonstrate, Stanley stuck his forefinger into his right ear and wiggled the digit. "Sometimes my hearing cuts out. I once slept through a Metallica concert. Front-row seats."

Kellaway stared at him. "Is that a fact." It wasn't a question.

"What?"

Kellaway started to repeat it, then stopped. Gave Stanley a go-to-hell look, then said, "Forget it. You didn't see anything, you didn't hear anything, you don't know anything, that about cover it?"

"That's right."

"Fine. If your memory comes back, give us a call." He handed Stanley a card. Shook his head in disgust again.

"Uh, sure."

With the door closed, Stanley went into a surge of panic. Coincidence. Had to be. He heard the noise last night and somehow assimilated it into his dream, that was it. Like when the phone sometimes rang and woke him up and he dreamed it was a school bell, he was late to class, he didn't have his homework done and didn't know any of the material on the test the teacher handed out, and he was naked, besides—

"Not now, Stanley," he told himself aloud. "If you don't get to work, you'll be looking for a job!"

But—what if it wasn't a dream?

He ran to the TV, grabbed the mask, ran to the sliding glass door that looked out on the rusted balcony. The grate would hold the weight of a couple of potted plants and maybe Milo. The one time

Stanley had dared to stand on it, the *skreech* of pro-
testing metal and oxidized bolts letting go had terri-
fied him. He managed to muscle the door open
wide enough to get his hand and the mask through,
then tossed the mask out. It hit the metal and
bounced into the air, went over the edge.

Good riddance.

He ran a fast shower—the water was still warm
when he shut it off, that's how fast it was—ran a
comb through his wet hair, and flew about getting
dressed. He was still using the electric razor as he
hurried into the kitchenette to pour fresh dog food
into the big feeder for Milo. "Gotta go, boy, I'm
late!"

But he couldn't find his keys. He looked everywhere. Finally he gave up. "Milo, keys!"

The dog leaped up and started sniffing around,
as if chasing a mouse. He grabbed the sofa cushion
and jerked it off, hopped up on the spring pad, and
rooted in the crack. Came up with Stanley's keys.

Stanley grabbed his briefcase. So he wasn't a
watchdog. He had his good points. "Good boy!
Gimme."

He grabbed the keys and scooted out the door.

Milo barked as he shut the door behind him.

In the hall, the Lieutenant and another plainclothes officer were talking to Mrs. Peenman while
a uniformed cop measured the holes in the floor
with a retractable tape.

Stanley paused to lock his door and he dawdled

a little, even though he was late, so he could over-
hear the conversation.

"Okay, let me be sure we've got this straight,"
Kellaway said. "Guy had a green head the size of a
pumpkin, wore a purple zoot suit and spats, and
was chasing an alarm clock with a big mallet."

"Sounds like my brother-in-law," the other cop
said.

"Yeah, mine, too," Kellaway said. "No offense,
lady, but you don't really expect us to swallow this,
do you?"

"Swallow it or choke on it. I saw what I saw."

"You drink a lot, Mrs. Peenman? Fond of cough
syrup?"

"I saw what I saw."

Stanley tried to get past without being noticed.

Mrs. Peenman said, "Where were you when all
this happened, Mr. Hero? You were still up, weren't
you? I heard the TV."

"I, uh, fell asleep watching it. Gotta go, I'm late
for work."

She glared at him as he sidled by.

Another uniformed cop holding a cell phone
scurried up. "Lieutenant? Watch commander wants
you over at a place called Ripley's Auto Repair."

Stanley gasped, but the sound apparently went
unheard.

"Why don't you tell the watch commander I'm
busy overseeing an investigation here?"

"Uh, he says it's related to this one, sir. Description of the perp matches."

Kellaway stared at a suddenly triumphant Mrs. Peenman. "See!"

Stanley kept moving, but slowly. He heard:

"Couple of guys got attacked. Pretty gruesome."

"They dead?"

"Probably wish there were, but no, un-uh."

Stanley made it to the hall's end and headed down the stairs. The elevator wasn't working and he was in too much of a hurry to risk it if it had been.

Stanley's bus happened to pass right by Ripley's Auto Shop. He didn't want to look, but the crowd gathered outside the yellow police tape spilled across the sidewalk and gawkers in their cars slowed down to see, too, so traffic was almost still. He had plenty of time. He couldn't *not* look.

Paramedics came out pushing two stretchers. The people on the bus gasped when they saw the two men on the stretchers: the pair had been spray-painted metallic blue and red, had hood ornaments glued to their foreheads, wire wheels stuck to their hands and feet. The paramedics had tried to cover them with sheets, but the two injured men, lying facedown, had something at least three feet tall tenting the covers in the region of their backsides.

Another gasp came from the bus passengers as one of the sheets caught in a stretcher wheel and was tugged off, to reveal the cause of the tenting effect: a muffler, the end of which was stuck into, well, the highly decorated man's own exhaust pipe.

Stanley stared in horror. It was Burt and Irv.

Just like in the dream. Which, obviously, had not been a dream at all. No way he could have incorporated *that* scenario into his nightmare.

He saw the lieutenant standing there, hands on his hips, looking disgusted. A young and attractive woman in her midtwenties walked up to where the policeman stood. She wore a blazer and jeans, carried a notebook, and was obviously trying to get the lieutenant to answer questions. A reporter. He wasn't having any of it, from what Stanley could see. The lieutenant waved the woman off.

Stanley watched her. She drifted toward the repair shop. When nobody seemed to be watching her, she ducked into the building.

Then the bus moved off and Stanley was left with his thoughts.

Whatever it was, whatever that mask had done to him, it was over. He'd thrown it away. Let that be the end of it. He wouldn't think about it anymore. It never happened. There was no way anybody who saw that goblin thing would ever be able to connect it to him. He was safe.

At the bank, Stanley hurried into his cubicle, clicked his computer on, hurriedly sat, and tried to look as if he'd been there for an hour.

Charlie, returning from the men's room, where

he'd probably been for the better part of an hour, saw him.

"My man. What happened to you last night? The girls and I looked for you, but you were gone. You get lucky elsewhere?"

"Yeah, lucky. You should have looked outside. I never made it past the Neanderthal on the door."

"Oh. Sorry about that. Too bad, Pebbles said she thought you were a real stud."

Stanley perked up a little. "Yeah?"

"Or a real dud. I'm not sure. It was kind of loud in there. Your girlfriend got a nice write-up, did you see?"

"Ipkiss!"

Stanley didn't need to turn to know who was yelling. Dickey, the smarmy son of the bank's owner and the world's worst boss. Dickey waddled into view and glared down at Stanley. "You were forty minutes late this morning. That's the same thing as stealing the bank's money, Ipkiss."

Well, son-of-a-gun, he'd come in early. Figured.

"Sorry, Mr. Dickey. It won't happen again. My car broke down." That was true enough, even though it hadn't happened today.

"No excuse. And if you weren't wasting your time ogling girlie pictures, you might get some work done." He snatched up the paper and looked at it.

"That's, ah, a prospective client of Stanley's, sir," Charlie put in. "She came in yesterday and got some information from him."

Well, bless you, Charlie.

"Oh, really? Well, next time she comes in, see that you send her to *my* office. We don't need our junior clerks scaring off lucrative business. These entertainers may be crude, but they have money. They need careful handling."

"Yes, sir," Stanley and Charlie echoed.

Dickey left. He took the paper with him.

"I wish my daddy owned a bank," Charlie said. "Then I could be a president like little Dickless there."

He looked down and saw in the open drawer a tissue with a big lipstick print on it. Stanley tried to close the drawer, but Charlie was faster. He snatched the tissue out. "Hello, what's this?"

"It fell in the drawer by accident. I, uh, forgot to throw it away."

"Stanley, Stanley. Forget about the singer. Girl like that is always looking for a MMTG man—more money than God. Ask her what her sign is, she'll probably say 'dollar.' "

Which would be better than my sign, Stanley thought. But he said, "You don't know that. She's an artist. Maybe she's not interested in material things. Maybe she's sensitive."

Charlie laughed. "Yeah, she can sense how much you have in your wallet at fifty paces. Face it, Stan-luigi, you need somebody more down-to-earth, somebody you can depend on, somebody like . . ."

He looked up and pointed at a red-haired

woman in a blazer and jeans asking one of the tellers something. He continued, ". . . somebody like her, for instance. Good-looking but not a knockout. Steady, honest, probably good with kids."

The auburn-haired woman turned and headed their way.

Charlie straightened his tie. "Only thing is, I saw her first, so she's mine."

Charlie would shove his dong into a hole in a tree if he thought there was a chance there might be a female squirrel in it.

The woman drew nearer.

Charlie said, brightly, "Hel-lo, ma'am. May I be of some assistance?"

"Stanley Ipkiss?"

Charlie's smile froze. He turned slightly and nodded at Stanley. Whispered, "So she's yours after all. Enjoy." He moved back to his desk. Stanley was pretty sure if he hadn't been there, Charlie would have pretended he was Ipkiss.

"I'm Stanley Ipkiss." He looked at the woman. She looked familiar. He'd seen her somewhere before. Recently, too. Where . . . ?

"I'm Peggy Brandt. With the *Star*."

"Hi. Uh, look, I had to cancel my subscription because the paper kept getting stolen. I'm sure it wasn't the paperboy's fault—"

"No, no, I'm not here about the subscription, Mr. Ipkiss. I'm a reporter. I wanted to ask you a couple of questions."

"Questions? About what?"

"You're a customer of Ripley's Auto Repair, aren't you?"

That's where he'd seen her. She was the woman talking to the lieutenant when Stanley's bus had gone past Ripley's.

Stall, Stanley.

"Me? No, I can't say that I am."

"Don't you own a green Civic?" She produced a work order coated with greasy fingerprints. That's what she'd been doing, sneaking into the shop past the police line.

"Oh, oh, yes. I had forgotten the name of the place. First time I ever went there. I only wanted an oil change, but there were some other repairs the car needed, so, yes, I guess you could call me a customer, even though I'm not a *regular* customer or anything."

Stanley, shut up! You're babbling!

Then: "Wait a second. You're Peggy Brandt? Of 'Ask Peggy'?"

She nodded. "That's right."

"Hey, I like your column. I sent you a letter last year. You printed it. 'Nice Guys Finish Last,' though I'm sure you don't remember."

"Whoa! You're Mr. Nice Guy? You know how much mail we got on that letter? There are hundreds of women out there looking for a man like you, Stanley. Why didn't you ever write back?"

He shrugged.

"You know how hard it is to find a decent guy in this town? If they aren't married and lying about it, they think monogamy is some kind of exotic hardwood."

Stanley was embarrassed. He hurried to cover it. "Well . . . why are you asking questions about a car-repair place?"

"Well, between you and me, 'Ask Peggy' pays dick, that's why. I'm trying to get a job as a real reporter, not just a sponge for lonely hearts to cry into. There was an assault and mayhem at the car place last night or early this morning. Could be a big story. Did you see anything suspicious when you were there? I won't use your name or anything, I just want to get the truth."

"I wish I knew the truth," he said. "But I don't think I can help you. It was just a ratty repair shop. I had a coupon for an oil change and it was on the way to work, only reason I went in."

Unless you count revenge-fantasy nightmares that turned out to be real.

Peggy nodded. "Ah, well. Too bad. Look, if you think of anything, give me a call." She handed him a card. "This is my *home* number." She stood.

"You really think there are hundreds of women in this town looking for a guy like me?"

"Sure do. I'm one of them. Call me sometime."

Dumbstruck, Stanley watched her leave. He didn't even think to smile until she was out the door.

How about that!

After she was gone, Charlie idled over to Stanley's desk. "Looked like you two hit it off."

"She seemed nice."

"Nice? Yeah, but she's got all the right equipment in the right places. You get her number?"

"As it happens, yes."

Charlie slapped him on the back. "Way to go, Stanleeto! That's the kind of woman you can take home to meet your mother. Better you should stay away from girls like Tina. You'll only get your fingers burned."

Stanley nodded absently. Maybe. And maybe a few burned fingers wouldn't be so bad, considering the prize he'd get to touch to earn them.

Better get to work. No point in giving Dickey any more ammunition.

7

Dorian sat at his desk playing with his new perpetual-motion machine. Five hundred bucks and change. Well, it wasn't *really* a perpetual-motion machine, according the the guy at Whiz Bang Electronics, even though that's what they called it. Perpetual meant forever. But what it was was pretty fun. You had a little steel spinner, like a kid's top, and a thick Pyrex glass case shaped like a tube, about as big around as a water tumbler and maybe twice as tall, mounted on a plastic base. What you did was, you spun the top on a magazine or something, then carefully loaded it into the side of the glass tube through a little door. There were magnets in the bottom and top of the tube, and when the top got inside, it floated in midair, balanced perfectly between the two magnets. But anybody could do that, there were little globes you could buy that did that. What this thing did was, once you got it inside, you closed the little door, which had a rubber seal around the edges, then you hit a switch on the base. A little pump went on and sucked all the air out of the glass case and made a vacuum inside. Well, not really a pure vacuum, the guy said, 'cause the top and a little bit of air were left inside, but enough so's the top would spin by itself for hours, 'cause it didn't have anything to rub against. Inertia, he said. Dorian vaguely remembered hearing something about that just before he'd dropped out of middle school to go to work for the Swede. It was why the Earth kept spinning after all these years. Nothing to slow it down much.

So far, Dorian's record on keeping the top spinning was nine hours and forty-three minutes.

He spun the top, hard, picked the magazine up, and urged the top into the cylinder. Shut the door, started the pump. After a minute the pump cut off and the one-way valve sealed the tube shut. He reached for the timer.

The phone rang.

"Somebody get that," he yelled.

He tapped the timer's start button.

The phone rang again.

"Is everybody *deaf* around here?"

But when he looked around, he didn't see Sweet Eddy or Orlando or Bobby or Nicky.

Where the hell *was* everybody?

He looked at the caller ID pad. Whoever was on the other end had entered a shutoff code. Damn.

He picked up the phone. "Yeah?"

"Why don't you come over and let's have a little talk?" the voice said. Then the caller hung up, leaving Dorian holding the phone. He cradled it. Wasn't any need for the speaker to say who he was.

It was the Swede.

Dorian's palms started to sweat.

He couldn't know, nobody but the Doctah and his boys knew and they wouldn't say anything, the Swede would kill them for knowing and not telling him sooner, they all knew that. It had to be about something else. Had to be.

What?

Well, whatever, he was going to have to go find out. The Swede had a whole list of things he didn't like, and being kept waiting was up there.

"Sweet! Orlando, dammit, where are you morons?"

Sweet stuck his head in through the doorway. "Yeah, boss?"

"Get the car. I feel like paying the Swede a little visit."

"Sure thing, boss. You want the Mercedes or the Cad?"

"The Cad." Hell, he was a loyal American, wasn't he? He liked to buy local stuff whenever he could, and while Detroit wasn't ever gonna catch up to the Germans, a Cad wasn't dog dung or anything.

* * *

Sweet drove, Orlando rode shotgun in the front of the powder-blue Caddy. In the back on the white leather seat, Dorian leaned forward and pulled his horsehide-and-sharkskin custom-made Kramer paddle holster from his waistband. He handed it and the piece in it over the front seat to Orlando.

"Don't you be dropping it or scratching it," he said.

The piece was a Smith & Wesson Ladysmith, a five-shot .38 snubnose with genuine registered ivory Spegel boot grips. The gun and holster and grips had set him back almost a thousand bucks altogether. He carried Glaser Safety Slugs in the little stainless-steel revolver, about as deadly a round as you could buy, least at close range. He knew that because there was this test they'd done on big goats somewhere, lined 'em up and blasted 'em, and the prefragmented slugs dropped them faster than anything else. 'Course the bullets weren't real accurate at long range, but he figured if he had to use the piece, it would be on somebody right in his face, so accuracy wasn't that big a deal.

He had a license, but if he had to shoot somebody, his lawyer had told him this particular gun and bullets would help make it court-proof. The lawyer said, "If you shoot somebody, you are gonna get sued, even if the cops don't hold you for criminal. You blast somebody with a Cobra or a Python and something like Black Talon ammo"— which they'd taken off the civilian market, it was so nasty—"and the jury is gonna look at you like you are a foaming-at-the-mouth serial killer. But if you do somebody with a *Lady*smith and safety slugs, why, how bad an hombre could you be?"

It made sense to Dorian, and besides, the Ladysmith was exactly the same as the Chief's Special, 'cept for cosmetic stuff and maybe a little easier trigger pull. Hell, if they made a gun called a Sissy and it shot Wimp ammo, he'd carry that.

He grinned.

The thing was, the Swede didn't allow anybody to bring guns into his place except his bodyguards. Had metal detectors set up to make sure, so Dorian would have to leave the piece in the car.

The Swede didn't know about the fiberglass CIA knife he carried in his sock, though. The detectors wouldn't pick that up. Push came to shove, Dorian was gonna have something to wave other than his smile.

Not that push would come to shove, not yet.

He hoped.

The Swede's place was in a high-rise he owned through some dummy corporation, and the place was all hand-rubbed teak and pecan and ebony, nothing but the best. He could afford it. Even if he changed all his loot into hundred-dollar bills, he had enough money to burn a herd of wet elephants—and then some.

With any luck at all, someday soon Dorian was going to have that kind of money. The Swede's money.

"Stay here," he ordered his bodyguards as they pulled up in front of the building.

He went through the first metal detector in the lobby. Took the elevator to the penthouse, where the second detector was backed up by a coffee-and-cream Jamaican woman bodybuilder who was beautiful, but whose arms were as big as Dorian's. Had a couple of black belts in something or the other, too. Dirisha was her name. Word was, she could tie a knot in you and bounce you like a basketball if she felt so inclined. Despite her looks, Dorian didn't like the idea of being with a woman who could throw him across the room if she got mad. He never hit on her, even though it would be good to have a spy in the Swede's nest.

"He's in the gym, mon," she said. "You go ahead on bock."

Dorian went through the anteroom to the Swede's private gym. Made the average Gold's look cheap, the Swede's training center did, and nobody but him and his guards ever even used it. Must have set him back four, five hundred thou to equip it. Hell, that was stamp money to the Swede, it fell out of his pocket, he might not bother to stoop to pick it up.

The Swede was lying on the bench-press bench, working with an Olympic bar loaded with chrome-plated rubber-rimmed free weights. Looked like four, five hundred pounds. He was doing reps. The Swede had blond hair, blue eyes, was as big as Bobby or Nicky, and according to what Dorian had heard, was stronger than either one of them. And him an old man, in his forties and all. He didn't do 'roids, though, he ate twigs and berries and crap like that. Took vitamins by the handful and swallowed them dry. Didn't smoke, didn't drink, but had himself plenty of women. Ate Kobi beef when he ate meat, flown in fresh from Tokyo the same day.

"Hello, Dorian," he said, not even breathing hard.

"Swede, hey, man. 's up?"

The Swede said, "You know what I hate?" He did another rep.

"Wind chimes."

"Besides that."

Dorian could rattle off fifteen or twenty things offhand, but that's not what the Swede wanted him to do. So he said, "I dunno, man."

"Losing, Dorian. I hate to lose."

He racked the barbell with a *clank* and sat up.

"I hear you, I hate to lose, too."

Another female jock walked into the room. This one was blond, tall, built like a diver. She carried a black silk robe and a black towel. The Swede took the towel and wiped his face with it, stood, and allowed the woman to slip the robe over his shoulders. He smiled at her, patted her on the butt, and she smiled back at him, then left.

"My smack and crack salesmen make a nice profit," the Swede said. "So do my call girls, my loan sharks, my poker parlors, and my gun smugglers. Everybody makes a profit who works for me except you, Dorian. My one legit business is losing money hand over fist. Why is that?"

"Hey, we've talked about this, man—"

"And we are talking about it again, *man*."

The Swede walked across the gym and through a door into one of his private offices. Dorian followed him.

The room's desk was made from a slab of shale, with computers built right into it. A map of Edge City with LED markers on it hung on the wall behind the desk. Each red dot was a place the Swede owned. The Swede slid into the handmade leather chair and looked up at Dorian. He didn't ask him to sit.

"Look, I got all kinds of high-visibility stuff coming down," Dorian said. "That highbrow charity thing of yours, half the town'll be there. We break even by this fall, early winter at the latest, and from then on, the place is a gold mine. It's already the freshest spot in town, people are lined up, throwing money at us."

"Then why isn't it sticking?"

"Expenses are high, Swede. You got to spend money to make money. Your man is doing the books, you see where every dime is going."

"Yeah, twenty grand a week worth of dimes, down the toilet. You'd better turn it around, Dorian. When the leaves start to drop from the trees, you'd better be coming to me with deposit slips, you understand? Or else you pick out the suit."

"What suit?"
"The one you get buried in."

In the car, Dorian was pissed.
"Gimme back my gun."

Orlando tendered the holster and Dorian slipped it back into his waistband, adjusted it so it was comfortable. Wasn't much to say to that kind of threat. He'd have to do that bank job. The Swede's accountant was too good, no way he could cook the books and get what he needed to buy himself an army. He was barely able to skim a thousand a week extra as it was. No, the bank would have to supply the cash. Once he got that, the Swede was gonna be laughing out the other side of his face.

"How'd it go, boss?" Sweet asked.

"Go? It went fine. The Swede loves me like a son. He just wanted to tell me I got a free hand with the club."

"That's good, ain't it?" Orlando said.

"Yeah, it's good."

Christ, he was gonna have to do that bank, if for no other reason than to hire help who had more brains than a Ritz cracker. Once that happened . . .

They'd see who picked out a suit then.

Stanley stood outside the Coco Bongo Club, resplendent in first-class Armani, with a ninety-dollar haircut, Gucci loafers, and a gold Rolex. It was raining, but the rain didn't seem to touch him.

A limo pulled up, stopped. The back door opened slowly. Tina stepped out.

She saw Stanley. Said, "Are you okay?"

"I am now," Stanley said, his voice an octave lower than usual. "Come over here, baby."

He could see her trying to resist, trying and failing. He was too powerful. He grinned.

"Why should I?"

"Because I want you to," he said.

"Oh, Stanley. I've been waiting for a man like you!"

She ran toward him. In slow motion. They embraced. Kissed passionately. Then she pulled back, grinned, and began to kiss his ear. To lick it.

Well, okay, if that was what turned her on . . .

"Oh, Stanley . . . !"

And of course, he woke up.

Milo was licking his ear.

"Jeez, Milo. Get off."

He sat up and rubbed at his eyes. He had taped the newspaper photo of Tina to his dresser. He stared at it. He had about as much chance with her as he did of flying to the moon by flapping his arms. Charlie was right. He wasn't ever going to set the world on fire, and women like Tina, they liked to stay hot.

He heard something. Couldn't place it, some kind of . . . well, it sounded like some kind of horn, like something the old Vikings would blow, *Ahhooo! Ahhooo!* but faint, in the distance. He turned around and walked toward the sliding glass door.

He stopped suddenly, as if he'd grown roots.

The mask. It was there, propped up against the outside of the glass door, looking at him.

How the hell—?

It couldn't be. He'd tossed it off the balcony, he'd *seen* it bounce over the railing and vanish from sight. It should have hit the street and been ground into wood pulp by the city traffic. *Adios, muchacho.*

He felt a deep fear rumbling in his belly, like a snake thrashing around, trying to escape.

Then he heard the voices. They were soft, but insistent, a chorus of almost musical whispers:

"Stanleeeey . . . Stanleeeeey . . ."

He shook his head.

Milo whined and ran under the bed.

Coming from the mask, the voices. It was calling to him.

"No. No way," he said.

"Stanleeeeeeey . . ."

"Forget it!"

He shook his head again. "Come *on*! That green goblin would scare a can of worms!"

Beauty is in the eye of the beholder, isn't it? The Mask has style. He's got class. He's funny. He's sharp. He's got the power. *Women like that more than looks. Anybody can get plastic surgery and look good, but power sucks them in every time.*

This was crazy. He was having a telepathic conversation with a piece of wood!

You know better than that, Stanley. You saw. You know.

Yeah. He licked his lips, lips suddenly gone dry as a summer desert.

He'd gone crazy before, but now that he knew what it was; now that he knew, he could control it. He could use the mask to augment himself, could throttle it down so he was in charge. He knew he could.

Well. At the very least there wasn't any point in leaving it out there on the balcony. Might as well bring it in. He didn't have to put it on.

He could just think about it.

He slid the glass door open. The motion knocked the mask over and it took a little hop toward the edge of the metal grate. No problem, he'd just step out and grab it.

He had one foot on the rusty metal and was reaching to collect the mask when the bolts holding the balcony to the brownstone sheared through, and the mask, the balcony, and Stanley all dropped toward the street.

Stanley screamed. He had his hand on the mask and there was only one way to save himself from being killed when he hit the concrete below. Only one way and the choice had been taken from him, if he wanted to live—

He jammed the mask onto his face.

Became the whirlwind and stopped falling.

Rose back toward his apartment and arrived therein, stopped his mad spin, and stood there in all his glory again.

The Mask was *back*.

From under the bed, Milo whined.

The Mask *zzzipped* into the bathroom and observed himself in the mirror. "Oh, you handsome devil, you!"

He sprouted a couple of extra arms and went into a frenzy of teeth brushing, cologne spraying, and batting himself with a powder puff.

"Howzabout a new color, hmm?"

The zoot suit ran through the spectrum. Turned yellow. A nice bright yellow, halfway between cartoon canary and champagne. "Yeah!"

Now he whipped out a matching yellow snap-brim fedora, cocked it on his head at a rakish angle, and smiled again. "S-s-s-smokin! Now, let's see, what else do we need?"

He pulled his zoot suit's pockets inside out. A moth fluttered up and flew away.

The Mask frowned. "Oops. Can't make the scene without any green. No dough, no go, no pay, no p-p-play!"

He smiled at the mirror. Got a glint off a front tooth. "Ah, well, it's the land of opportunity, isn't it? Money, money everywhere!"

And where, he thought, would be a perfect place to score some bread? A place where they kept it in bunches, and a place that surely owed him a lot more than they'd been paying him, hmm? It was only fair, right?

He shot out of the bathroom and headed for the front door.

Milo whined.

"Don't wait up, puppy, I might be late!"
He opened the door and *zzzippped* away.
He was back!
Hahahahahaaaaa!

8

From the outside, the truck looked like a medium-sized Dipsy Doodle Diaper Service van where it sat parked on the street in front of the Edge City First Bank.

Inside, the van's walls were stacked with high-tech electronics: computers, cameras, monitors, ultrasonic and laser devices. Doctah Freeze, Sweet Eddy, and Orlando, dressed all in ninja black except for their faces, checked their weapons. Even Freeze had a piece, a nine, though he didn't look too comfortable with it.

Through a hole in the floor of the van, Sweet worked on a bundle of wiring pulled up from the conduit in the manhole below the truck.

Sweet mumbled, "White . . . green . . . blue—here is it, Doc."

"Just a second." Freeze looked up. "Yo, you there?"

In his office, watching on his monitor, Dorian said, "I'm here, man." He could see everything going on in the van, plus Orlando and Sweet had wide-angle minicams in their belt buckles and Dorian could switch the view to those, if he wanted to, and see *every*thing as it went down. Man, it sure was great living here in the future.

Freeze pressed his wireless earphone with one finger so he could hear better. "We done cut the outside lines. Soon as I bypass that local alarm circuit, we head in," he said.

"Maybe this would be a good time for me to go circulate and be seen in the club, then."

"Come back in five minutes, you can watch me peel that vault like an orange. The *Doc*tah is about to operate." He wiggled his fingers.

"Five minutes. I'll be back." Dorian smiled and stood. They didn't use names on the air, but it wouldn't have mattered if they did, 'cause the signal was scrambled. Freeze said nobody could decode it unless they were an electronic genius, and even then, it would take a while and they wouldn't be on the air that long. Freeze knew his stuff.

Dorian was about to leave when he heard an alarm whine from the monitor and Freeze said, "Shit, fool, what you doin'?"

Sweet said, "Nothing, man, I didn't even touch it."

Dorian reached for the volume control. "Freeze? What's going on there?"

"Hell if I know. The bank's audible just went off, but we ain't done that wire yet. We cut the phone link to the cops, but somebody passin' by might hear that noise. Come on, we better check this out!" Freeze waved them through the van's sliding door.

Dorian cursed and fumbled with the camera controls. It took a couple of tries to switch the POV to Sweet's belt cam. He could smell his own sweat, a sour stink that cut through the deodorant he wore. Damn.

The bouncing motion as Sweet ran toward the bank's front door made Dorian want to heave, but after a second Sweet slid to a stop.

"Get to the sides," Freeze ordered. "I'm gonna pick the lock."

He dropped his knees, inserted a pickgun into the keyhole—

The door exploded outward, a whirlwind knocked Freeze on his ass, then whipped out of sight.

What the hell . . . ?

Sweet and Orlando uttered a few choice curses, including a couple of twelve-letter ones, and turned enough so they could see what looked like a pocket-sized yellow tornado moving back and forth in the street.

Jesus and All the Little Angels. What was *that*?

The tornado spun back toward the surprised trio. Came to a stop, and—

Turned into a troll in a yellow zoot suit with a matching hat.

For a second Dorian thought maybe the TV signal had gotten crossed somehow. Looked like a frog on steroids standing there, grinning like a baboon.

Dorian stared. He could only imagine what Sweet, Orlando, and Freeze must feel like.

The green-headed guy had three huge sacks slung over one shoulder, like Santa Claus, and as Dorian watched, the guy reached up into the air with his free hand and grabbed what looked like several twenties floating down like leaves. "Oops, I don't want to be a litterbug, now, do I? Saaay, would you guys hold my money for a second?"

With that, he thrust the sacks one at a time at the three men.

Sweet's sack blocked his camera. Dorian cursed and switched to Orlando's cam, which wasn't covered—

Just in time to watch the guy in the mask reach out and slap Freeze's face, *whap-whap!* like Moe doing Curly. He repeated the move on Sweet, and though Dorian couldn't see it, he heard the double slap as he did Orlando, too.

The guy grabbed the sacks, slung them over his shoulder, tipped his hat, waggled his eyebrows into huge wrinkles, and vanished with a sound like a cartoon gunshot ricochet.

Holy shit!

Freeze pulled his nine and opened up. Put

twelve or fifteen rounds in the air, ran dry, started yelling. "Get 'im!"

Sirens screamed.

"Cops!" Orlando yelled.

"Boogie!" Sweet hollered.

What the *hell* was going on here?

He heard the cops yelling for them to halt, heard them open up with their guns. Watched the picture bounce wildly as they ran.

Holy—!

The limo pulled up in front of the Coco Bongo and it was the biggest limo anybody had ever seen. Not just a stretch, but a stretched stretch. The passenger door arrived, opened, and The Mask rolled out on a chrome-plated Harley, a vintage XLCH, dressed like Marlon Brando in *The Wild One.*

The crowd parted like the Red Sea. The Mask pulled the hog to a stop in front of the bodybuilder with his admit list. The Mask hopped off the bike, twirled in a balletlike two-second blur, and stopped, again in the yellow suit and fedora. Walked up to the muscle man.

"Hi there, Booby."

"That's, uh, Bobby. Uh, uh, are you on the, uh, list—Mr., uh—?"

Which was as far as old Bobby Booby got. With a fencer's lunge that would have done credit to Zorro, The Mask bent-the-knee and shoved a fist-thick wad of cash into Booby's gaping maw, chok-

ing off any further comments. Said, "Great to see
you, too, Booby. My best to Ahnahld."

Then The Mask did a little jitterbug-bop number
past Booby and into the club.

Tina took the stage, accompanied by a drumroll
rimshot and a splash of hot-pink lighting. She
smiled and undulated her way to the old forties ra-
dio-style stand-up mike. She wore a gown that was
all mesh and sequins and left little to the imagination.

Dorian, troubled over the snafu at the bank, allowed himself to be ushered to his private table
down front. Whatever happened with the heist, he
needed to be seen in public miles away when it went
down. He nodded at Tina, knowing she probably
couldn't see him for the spotlight in her face.

Up in one of the real banyon trees growing from
the huge pots, one of the tropical birds—a trained
parrot or a macaw, Dorian never could tell them
apart—gave a long wolf whistle.

The crowd laughed. It was a great setup.

A new waitress in a tight leopardskin-print leotard put a glass of Southern Comfort over ice on the
table in front of Dorian. "Here you go, Mr. Tyrel."

He looked at her. She had a great figure. Big
hooters, naturals, too. He gave her a smile. "Thanks,
honey. You call me Dorian, though. All the girls
do."

She smiled back. He'd see her later, for sure. He
picked up his drink and took a big sip. Maybe

Freeze would catch the guy who robbed the bank.
He shook his head. What were the odds of that?
That some fool would hit the same bank on the
same night, five minutes ahead of Dorian's men?
Crazy world.

Onstage, Tina did a talk-sing intro to her song.

Love makes me treat you the way that I do
Gee Baby ain't I good to you
There's nothing too good for a boy that's so true
Gee Baby ain't I good to you

The band slid in, low horns and growling saxes,
and Tina went into the torch song "Gee Baby Ain't
I Good to You." The crowd whistled and clapped.
She gave them a few bars, then came down off the
stage and started to work the tables, the spot staying
with her but the houselights going dim.

I know how to make a good man happy
I'll treat you right
With lots of lovin'
Just about every night

The Mask saw her come down off the stage and
his eyes shot out on long stalks, his heart stretched
two feet out of his of chest and thumped wildly,
and an *aahhooggaa!* horn played from under his hat
on the table.

Mama mia!

The customers at the nearby tables stared at him

as steam hissed out of his ears. He didn't care. She was a' some spicy meatball!

He watched her walk across the floor.

> Love makes me treat you the way that I do
> Gee Baby ain't I good to you

Dorian felt a presence at his elbow. He turned. Sweet Eddy. Looked like six miles of bad road.

"Did you get the money?"

"Not exactly."

If looks could have killed, Sweet Eddy would be a smoking blob on the rug. "Where is Freeze?"

"Upstairs. He, uh, took a bullet from the cops."

"Let's go." Dorian stood and straightened the lapels of his jacket. Took a last look at Tina and followed Sweet out of the room.

> They got me paying taxes for what I gave to you
> Gee Baby ain't I good to you

The song done, Tina took a bow.

The crowd roared its approval.

So did The Mask. His face stretched out, turned into that of a cartoon wolf. He howled, stamped his foot like a belly-scratched dog, pounded on the table, and ended with a wolf whistle that blew several of the live tropical birds right out of the potted trees.

Hubba, hubba!

The Mask sprang up, blurred around the perimeter of the room, and leaped onto the piano. He snapped his fingers and a baby spotlight hit him.

"What say we *rock* this joint?" With that, he jumped down next to the startled pianist, grabbed the man's tux, and spun him on his stool. When he stopped spinning, the man was transformed into a beatnik be-bopper, complete with Vandyke beard, beret, and a black turtleneck sweater. He hit the keys with both hands and began pounding out a mean boogie-woogie.

The Mask plucked a conductor's baton from the air and turned to face the rest of the orchestra. Like the piano player, they changed from sedates in tuxes to swinging hipsters. The music heated up to a driving prerock boogie behind the piano.

"Now, *that's* more like it!" The Mask yelled. He leaped high into the air, did a double front flip, and came down in front of Tina.

"Let's cut a rug, honey!"

He grabbed her hand and they went into an impossible dance routine. He lifted her, threw her, twirled her, all the time keeping a backbeat jitterbug going like stink. He moved like a cross between Baryshnikov and Gumby, twisting, dropping into full splits, spinning like a top, handling Tina with the greatest of ease. She was right there with him. Of course.

"Now we're s-s-smokin!"

They danced like maniacs on the floor, the tables, even on a couple of chairs, The Mask and Tina.

And the crowd went wild.

Dorian and Sweet went into the office. Freeze looked bad. Orlando had a wadded-up shirt pressed against Freeze's back.

"What the hell happened?" Dorian demanded.

"I'll be cut up and sold for pork chops if I know," Freeze said. He sounded weak. "This guy comes out of the bank in a mask, lookin' like Frankenstein's worst nightmare, slaps us around, and hauls ass with three big bags of cash. Somebody musta called it in, or the cops musta heard the alarm, even though we'd cut the phone lines."

"The guy disappeared into thin air, boss," Orlando said. "One second he was right there in my sights and I was about to plink him, the next second . . . poof!"

"I got your poof right here," Dorian said. "You bunch of clowns let some dickhead in a cartoon mask waltz in and take *my* money? Why am I paying you?"

"The Doctah needs a real doc, boss," Orlando said.

"What I need is a cigarette," Freeze said.

Dorian pulled a nail from his pack and put it between the man's lips. Lit the end. Waited for Freeze to toke on it. The butt fell from his lips and Freeze slumped forward.

"Freeze?"

"He's dead, boss," Orlando said, his fingers on the man's neck.

"Son-of-a-*bitch!* I want the guy who did this!

You hear me? If you got to track him to the ends of the earth, I want him!"

Sweet said, "I don't think we'll have to go that far."

Dorian turned and glared at Sweet. "What!"

Sweet pointed at the monitor. The main room downstairs. "That's him, boss. Right there, dancing."

Dorian stared. "Here? In the club? He takes my money and then he's got the balls to walk right into my club? He's dead meat!"

He pulled his snubnosed revolver.

"Come on. We're going to get my money and we're going to make this sucker sorry he was ever born!"

They started for the door.

9

The Mask and Tina slid across the cleared floor—
nobody else was bothering to dance, not with this
kind of show right in front of them—and Tina's
heels left smoking tracks.

The crowd went wilder yet.

The pair of them together made the best 1940s
jitterbug movie look sick.

The Mask shoved Tina between his legs and did
a front flip, held on, and twisted himself inside out.
Came down facing her, holding both hands. His
body was almost still, but his feet jittered and jived
as he smiled at her.

This was how to dance!

The crowd practically elected him President.

The band headed for the finale. The Mask spun
Tina around and around his body like a Hawaiian
fire dancer's baton. She was a gymnastic blur.

The band hit the final bar and held it.

The Mask screeched Tina to a halt, grabbed her, bent her over backward, and nailed her with a Valentino kiss. It blew her shoes off with a mortar's *whoosh*.

Now, *that* was how to *end* a dance—

"Everybody out!" somebody yelled.

A gun went off.

A bullet clipped a piece of The Mask's tie off as neatly as a tailor's scissors. The tip of the tie fluttered to the floor and morphed back into material from Stanley's pajamas. He stared at the bit of cloth. Talkin' *uggglllly*!

"Incoming!" The Mask yelled. He straightened Tina up, then shoved her behind him. Turned to face the shooter.

The crowd mooed like cowboy movie cattle and stampeded for the exits.

In fifteen seconds the place was empty—save for The Mask, Tina, and three guys with guns.

The Mask looked at the man with the still-smoking gun. "Hi, fellas. Looks like you're wallflowers—the dance is over."

"Dorian!" Tina said.

Dorian swaggered over to where the couple stood. "All right, twinkle toes, I want to know where my money is and I want to know where it is *now*!"

The Mask grinned, whipped out a green eyeshade, manifested sleeve garters and a puffy striped shirt, and came up with an old mechanical pull-handle hundred-key calculator.

"Okkkay, lemme see. . . ." He punched the keys and pulled the handle, got a nice *ka-ching!*

"Hmm. Looks like seventeen-five percent in T-bills, eight and three quarters in stocks and bonds, carry the one, and divided by the gross national product—"

Ka-ching! Ka-ching!

"You ought to diversify more, Dorian. Get into some pork-belly futures."

"That's it," Dorian said. "Put one in his knee-cap, Sweet."

Sweet lifted his pistol and pointed it at The Mask.

Popped off a round—

The Mask leaped, spun, did a plié and came down *en pointe,* dressed in a pink tutu and matching toe shoes, with a long pink wig.

The bullet went wide.

"Say, honey, you got a cigarette?" the ballerina asked.

Sweet frowned, shot again.

The Mask spun, came out of it as a matador in a full suit of lights, cape flaring in a perfect veronica as the bullet went past.

"Olé—!" He said. A rose appeared, the long stem gripped in his teeth. He waggled his eyebrows. *"Tengo cigarillo, amigo?"*

"Hold still!" Sweet yelled, and let go another round.

The Mask spat out the rose, morphed into a Russian Cossack dancer, and saber-kicked over the slug's path.

"Hey!" he hollered. "*Papirósa*, comrade?"

He leaped, did a full layout gainer, came down as a cowboy, plucked a lit cigarette from the air. Stuck it into his mouth, dragged on it. "Ah, there it is, thanks, podnah—"

Sweet fired.

The Mask grabbed his chest. He blew a thick cloud of blue smoke out in a single puff.

Dorian said, "The knee, fool! The *knee*!"

"Arrgghh! Yuh got me, pard!" He slumped forward, threw his arms around Sweet, and slithered down him to the floor, burbling as he went. Spat out the cigarette.

Sweet looked surprised. He knelt next to the bleeding cowboy.

"Tell . . . tell Auntie Em to take care of Old Yeller," The Mask said.

He coughed and sprayed Sweet with blood. "And—and . . . Toto, too."

He gave a liquid wheeze. "Tell . . . Tiny Tim I'm sorry I'll miss . . . Christmas. Tell Scarlett I really *do* give a damn. . . . Oh, Sweet, it's gettin' dark, I'm afraid, Sweet, hold me, I'm goin' to the last roundupppp. . . ."

Another cough, another spew of blood, and The Mask went limp. His long pink tongue flopped from the side of his mouth.

Sweet blinked. "Aw, gee," he said. He got teary-eyed. "I was aimin' at his knee!"

Everybody stared down at the dead man.

Suddenly a cartoon audience popped into being all around them, applauding and cheering wildly. The Mask opened one eye. An arm that had to be thirty feet long stretched in from nowhere and thrust an Oscar at The Mask. He leaped up, grabbed the Oscar, began bowing to the thunderous applause. His cowboy clothes shimmered and changed into an evening gown that Cher would lust after. "Thank you! Thank you! You *like* me! You really *like* me! I'd like to mention a few people—" He pulled a toilet paper roll of a list from his bosom. It unwound, hit the floor, and rolled out the nearest exit. The list had thousands of names on it.

"My mom, my dad, my fat sister Louise, my favorite uncle Lou—"

Dorian growled and pointed the snubby at The Mask. Started shooting.

The Mask did a cartoon-voice *whoo-whoo!* and bounced away like a demented pogo stick fueled by nitro and speed.

Dorian started shooting, as did Sweet and Orlando.

Suddenly the club's doors flew open and a horde of cops burst in.

"Nobody moves!"

Dorian squatted slowly and carefully and put his piece on the floor. He didn't want to drop it and scratch the ivory. When he came up, he saw that Sweet and Orlando had also unhanded their guns.

The green guy was nowhere in sight.

Lieutenant Kellaway glided in past the clot of uniforms and stopped in front of Dorian. "Little target practice, Tyrel?"

Dorian shrugged. "It's my club. I can do what I want inside."

"Yeah, but you can't do it outside, pal."

"You got a warrant, Kellaway, or did you just stop by to chat?"

"I got probable cause. A couple of guys answering the description of your boys were spotted knocking over the Edge City First Downtown Branch this evening. They headed this way."

One of the uniformed cops started to frisk Dorian. "Easy, junior. You're gonna give me a woody and you ain't my type."

Kellaway waved the uniform off. "I know all about Moe and Larry here," he said, nodding at Sweet and Orlando. "But since when did you start recruiting little green men from Mars, Tyrel?"

"Barking up the wrong tree, Lieutenant. I know about the guy in the mask, but he ain't mine. You any kind of a cop, you'd know that, too. Be out looking for him instead of harassing me."

"This isn't harassment, Tyrel. Here, let me show what harassment looks like. Search the place, boys."

The cops went into a feeding frenzy that would shame a school of great whites swimming in pure blood. They tipped over, pulled up, and otherwise knocked the furniture and fixtures every which way.

Nobody said anything for a few minutes while the cops wrecked the club. Finally Dorian said, "You never learn, do you? You know why you don't make Captain, Kellaway? 'Cause I got friends up so high they can give you a nosebleed just to kiss their boots."

Kellaway grinned, and hit Dorian with a short jab to the face. The punch rocked him, but he wouldn't give the bastard the satisfaction of going down. He put his hand to his face and it came away bloody.

"Well, what do you know," Kellaway said. "Looks like those nosebleeds are contagious, don't it?"

"You're gonna be sorry for that, Kellaway. Real sorry."

A uniform came down the stairs. "Lieutenant? There's a stiff upstairs. Looks like Wilo Jenkins, aka Doctah Freeze."

"My, my. That doesn't look too good for the home team, does it, Tyrel?"

"I didn't shoot him. None of my boys did. Ballistics will prove it. And they didn't rob no bank. You won't find any evidence to support that one, either."

"Turn around and put your hands behind you, Tyrel. We're going to go downtown and have us a little visit, you and I and Laurel and Har-har there."

Dorian said, "Tina, call the lawyer."

"Better call a magician, too, honey," Kellaway said as he snapped his cuffs on Dorian. "He's gonna need Houdini to get his natty butt out of this one."

As they started to leave, Kellaway bent and picked something up from the floor and frowned at it. Dorian didn't get a good look, but it seemed to be a scrap of ugly cloth, flannel or something, in a putrid paisley.

Dorian was pissed. The Swede wasn't gonna be happy having to shell out to repair the damage the fuzz had just done, that green bastard had gotten away clean, and the sucker still had *his* money.

Not a real good day, all things considered.

Stanley woke up and saw Milo standing next to the bed. The dog had the Frisbee in his mouth, but he was also growling. Now what?

Stanley sat up. He felt like hell. Where were his pajamas? He was exhausted, too, and little wonder. He looked at the mask. It was on the pillow next to him. That would be what Milo was grumbling about. He didn't blame him.

Another session or two like last night and he'd burn up like a meteor hitting the atmosphere at speed. But he'd danced with Tina, and once she'd gotten over her initial shock, she'd liked it. She smiled, that must mean something, right?

Right.

He ambled into the bathroom and examined his face in the mirror. He looked as bad as he felt. There were dark bags under his eyes big enough to pack laundry in. Jeez.

Somebody pounded on the door. Stanley jumped.

"Open up, Ipkiss! It's the police!"

Kellaway. He recognized the voice.

He ran to the bed, grabbed the mask, and headed for the closet. It didn't really look like The Mask, no more than he did, but there wasn't any point in giving the cops any ideas.

When he opened the closet, an avalanche of paper money fell on him. He could smell it, nothing quite had that same scent as a big bunch of paper currency.

The bank!

"Open up, Stanley! I can hear you in there!"

He had to do something, fast!

"I don't have any clothes on! Lemme get a robe, be right with you!"

He used the Frisbee to shovel the money back into the closet.

More pounding.

"I'm coming!"

He got most of the money back into the closet, threw the mask and the Frisbee in after it, then swept the rest of the bills under the bed. Ran for the door. Grabbed his bathrobe off the wall hook.

Opened the door.

"What's up, Lieutenant? I'm kind of in a hurry—"

Kellaway barged in past him.

"Won't you come in?"

"Nice of you to ask. I got some questions for you, pal. You got some explaining to do."

Milo was at the closet door, scratching on it. Damned dog wanted his Frisbee. "Milo, quit it."

The dog whimpered.

"Let's cut to the chase, Ipkiss. Where were you last night?"

"Uh, here . . . mostly. Something wrong?"

"Wrong? Why, no, other than the brass is gonna whip my tail with an ugly stick if I don't catch this Mask character who's dumping all over my city. What do you know about him?"

"Mask? Me? Nothing."

"Ipkiss, I've had a very long night. I had to watch as a very bad guy and his hired thugs got cut loose after a song and dance by a high-priced mouthpiece. I got a dead guy, a robbed bank, and mechanics who are sending some proctologist's kids to Harvard. Don't insult me. This Mask was seen in this building, then he hit the bank where you work and then I found *this* at the Coco Bongo, where, according to witnesses, the same green goon did a dance number that made Fred Astaire in his prime look like nothing."

He waved a scrap of cloth under Stanley's nose

"Tell me there are two idiots who have pajamas with this pattern mixed up in all this."

Milo yapped at the closet door. Scratched at it with both paws.

"Milo, get away from the door or I'll kill you,"

Stanley said, smiling through gritted teeth at the dog.

Milo backed away, darted under the bed.

"How about you let me see those pjs, Ipkiss?"

"I—I would, but, uh, I can't. When I got home from work yesterday, somebody had—had, uh, broken into my apartment and swiped some of my stuff. Including my, uh, pajamas."

Kellaway stared at him. "Somebody stole your pajamas."

"Uh, yeah, that's right. Terrible when the city is so bad a crook will swipe a man's nightclothes."

"Did you report it?"

"I meant to."

Kellaway sniffed the air loudly, once, twice, thrice. "Smell that?"

"Sometimes the dog gets gas," Stanley began.

"No, it's not gas, it's *bullshit*! I hate that smell." He glared at Stanley, began to punch him on the chest with his forefinger, punctuating his words as he spoke: "Don't . . . leave . . . town, Ipkiss. Because you and I, we're gonna talk again. Soon. Real soon. And I'm gonna get all the answers I want, do you understand?"

Stanley stared as the Lieutenant marched to the door, opened it, and slammed it behind him.

The closet door sprang open and the money cascaded out again.

Milo ran out from under the bed and dug through the bills, found the Frisbee. Came over to

Stanley with the plastic disk in his mouth, tail wagging.

"Milo, what am I going to do? I'm in trouble!"

Dorian watched the green guy zigzagging around the inside of the bank like Mercury on crank. He shook his head.

"He ain't human, boss," Orlando said.

Dorian was inclined to agree, except that he never agreed with anything Orlando said as a matter of principle. God knew what that would lead to. Orlando might get to thinkin' he had a brain. "He's human. He's on dust or speed, wearing a bulletproof vest or something."

One of the Swede's bought-and-paid-fors in the police department had dubbed a copy of the bank's surveillance camera's tape of the robbery and gotten it to Dorian. He also had a copy of the preliminary report from Kellaway's team. No prints on any of Dorian's crew, one of the reasons they had to let them go, plus no eyewitnesses. The cops couldn't link him to this clown. He'd told the cops that Freeze showed up, wounded, and if he'd been involved in the heist, well, that was his business and none of theirs. Freeze wasn't around to say any different and he had Sweet and Orlando to swear it, plus a club full of witnesses who had seen him watching Tina sing when the cops were shooting at the robbers.

Tina now sat on the gray leather couch painting her nails. Sweet was on the cell phone making calls.

"Okay, here's the deal," Dorian said. "Fifty grand to the guy who delivers The Mask to me, preferably alive, before the cops get him. I want him yesterday, I'll settle for tomorrow. Put the word out to every junkie, working girl, dealer, everybody. I will consider it a personal favor and I will owe whoever comes up with superfrog a large one to go with the cash. Go."

Orlando and Sweet left.

Dorian gave Tina a sour look. "What are you staring at?"

"You. You losing it, Dorian?"

"I ain't losing *nothin'*. Maybe some extra baggage I don't need."

"Meaning?"

"You didn't seem to be putting up much of a fight last night when you were dancing with The Mask."

"You saw how he was. If you and Sweet and Orlando couldn't handle him, you think *I* had a choice?"

"I don't know, baby. Maybe you didn't. And maybe you did."

He stepped behind the couch and toyed with her hair. "But when this is all done and this Mask idiot is history, anybody who crossed me gets payback. Anybody."

He meant it, too. Anybody.

She held her fingers up, inspected the nails. Turned and looked up at him. "Aw, honey, you know I wouldn't cross you. I know which side of my bread is buttered."

He nodded and turned away. He believed that. She was too smart to do anything that stupid. 'Course, that was one of the problems with smart women, and smart men, too. You didn't want them so stupid; then again, you didn't want them too sharp, 'cause then they might start getting ideas. He didn't want to find himself in the Swede's position a few years down the road, with some ambitious employee thinkin' to take him out. No, it was a tricky balance, the people you had working for you. He'd have to pay careful attention to that when he took over. Real careful attention.

He walked away from the couch. Saw that his perpetual-motion machine was still spinning along. Inertia, that was the key. He had to get things moving in the right direction. Once that happened, they'd roll along just fine.

"Tell you what, Tina, my love. You see this character again, I want to hear about it in a hurry. He seems to like you. You keep him busy until I can collect him, why I might be able to see my way to givin' you that fifty grand."

He waited for her to say something.

"If I see him, I'll hold him for you, Dorian. You don't have to pay me anything. You take good care of me."

Just the right thing to say, Smart.

Maybe too smart . . .

10

There was a crowd at the bank when Stanley arrived, customers worried about their deposits. He shook his head as he worked his way through the milling throng. What kind of idiots were these people? Didn't they know their money was insured? Were they so stupid they thought that when they came in for a withdrawal, the bank was going to give them the exact same dollar bills they'd deposited? Did they maybe have some kind of serial-number fetish?

He made it to his desk. He wasn't being very charitable in his thoughts. Truth was, he didn't feel much of the milk of human kindness at the moment. He had missed as much of his beard as he'd hit with the razor this morning, his jacket was wrinkled—hell, his *face* was wrinkled—and he knew he looked like somebody with a bad hangover. And he felt worse. This Mask business was very, very . . . draining.

Yes, technically, he supposed it was his fault these people were here clogging up the bank's lobby like a greasy old hairball in a sink, but his only crime had been to put the mask on. And that wasn't even a crime. He'd just wanted to impress Tina. He was kind of like a horse The Mask rode, that wasn't him doing all that stuff, it wasn't him, even though he was there.

He didn't think it was. It was hard to be sure.

He managed a creaky grin. Well. He was pretty sure he had impressed Tina. That business of blowing her shoes off when he kissed her, that was a neat touch. Whoever he became when he was The Mask, he had a lot more style and panache than Mr. Milquetoast Stanley had ever dreamed of having—

"Ipkiss, you idiot! We're having a crisis and you come waltzing in here almost an hour late! Who the hell do you think you are?"

Something deep inside Stanley groaned sharply. He turned to see Dickey glaring at him. Behind him, Charlie and a couple of the tellers watched in fascinated horror. He was about to get reamed and nobody wanted to get too close, it might splatter on them.

"This is it, this is the last straw, Ipkiss! No more Mr. Nice Guy!"

Nice Guy? Dickey?

Whatever it was that had groaned in Stanley now screamed.

And snapped.

The little twerp was right about one thing, though. It *was* the last straw. The rage that had simmered in Stanley all of his life, never escaping except when freed for a few hours by The Mask, blew out of him like Mount St. Helens freeing her deadly stone winds:

"Back off, Dickey!"

If Stanley had turned into a werewolf and started howling, he couldn't have surprised the onlookers any more. Especially Dickey. The man's eyes went wide. He started to speak, but Stanley headed him off.

"How would you like it if I put a bug in your old man's ear? Told him exactly how you use this place like your personal piggy bank? About the little end runs you've done on the corporate auditors *and* the IRS? How would you like to spend your summer vacation for the next five years at Club Fed? I know where the loans are buried, *Mister* Dickey, and I can dig them up just like that!" He snapped his fingers.

It sounded like a pistol shot in the sudden silence.

Dickey's face morphed from outrage to terror faster than a flea's orgasm. He sputtered, couldn't find any words. Managed: "Ah-ah-ah!"

"So here is the deal: Leave me alone or I will nail your hide to the nearest wall, and use it for a dartboard!"

Dickey looked as if he had been blindsided by

the entire Dallas Cowboy front line, as if he had been hit full force in the face by the giant killer surf off the point in Makaha.

Hahahahahahaaa! Wipeout!

A tiny voice deep in Stanley's psyche said, *Yesss!*

Oh, despite the danger, it felt good to do that. Yes *sir*!

His boss managed to wave one hand in a kind of spastic denial. Finally found language again. "Oh. Oh. Never mind. That's, that's all. We won't speak of this again. Ah, g-g-go on about your work." He turned and tottered off, and if not a broken man, certainly bent in new and unusual ways.

My God, his father had been right. If you stand your ground and fight back, sometimes the bully will go away instead of wiping up the floor with you. Amazing.

Charlie came over and a new respect shone from his eyes. "Stanley? What side of whose bed did *you* wake up on this morning? That was magnificent!"

Stanley shook his head. He felt a twitch, and his face contorted for a second, so fast he thought he might be imagining it. He couldn't see it, but it felt as if his flesh were mimicking that of The Mask's features. A beat, and the feeling passed.

"Whoa, Stan! You okay?"

"I haven't been myself lately," he said.

"You look like hell, too. You need to loosen up more, Stanlureeno. Tell you what. I got a couple of tickets to that gangsters' major charity ball at the

Coco Bongo Saturday night. Anybody who is any-body'll be there. Want to go?''

The Coco Bongo. A place of mixed memories, that.

"I dunno, Charlie. Maybe."

He looked up, saw Tina working her way through the crowded lobby. Felt a sudden lift in his spirits. Could it be that the gods would grant him *two* miracles in one day? "Excuse me a second."

Charlie saw Tina approaching. "Ah. You got a secret you aren't letting me in on, pal?"

"Go away, Charlie."

Charlie grinned and moved toward his desk. He bowed to Stanley, hands pressed together in *namaste*. "To hear is to obey, Sahib."

Tina arrived.

"Hi."

"Hi."

"Come to finish the paperwork?"

"Uh, well, no, not actually. I just wanted to let you know I, uh, won't be opening an account here after all. Sorry."

Stanley's spirit sagged. "Oh? May I ask why? It wasn't the robbery, was it?"

"No, nothing like that."

"Anything wrong? Anything I can do?"

She gave him a little smile. "Why would you care, Stanley?"

"How could I not?"

Her smile increased a little. "You're sweet."

It was like a fiery lance through his heart. The

dreaded "sweet." Next she was going to tell him he reminded her of her little brother. But he pressed on. "I'd really like to help."

"Well, I'm thinking about leaving the club. It's kind of a bad situation there. And I might have to, you know, leave town to get work."

"Come on. I've heard you sing. You're terrific."

"Talent is only a little piece of it. You have to have an angle and who you know is as important as what you can do. You get on the wrong side of certain people in this city and work gets hard to find. It isn't an easy business."

"Believing in yourself never is," he said.

She regarded him with a quizzical expression, as if seeing him for the first time.

"Yeah. Well, anyway, thanks for the help. Maybe another time. Just thought I'd let you know." She started to leave. Paused. "You know that guy who supposedly robbed the bank?"

He stiffened. "The Mask? What about him?"

"Does anybody have any idea who he is? I mean—"

"Why do you want to know?"

"Oh, no reason. Just curious. I, ah, met him at the club last night." She turned away again.

Don't let her go, you moron! Say something to keep her here!

He said, "You liked the guy?"

She paused again. "You know, it's funny, but, yeah, I kinda did."

"With a face like that? It would scare his own mother."

"Didn't you see the *Phantom*?" she said. *"Beauty and the Beast*? Looks aren't everything."

"You interested in the guy? Even though he's a bank robber?"

He had her full attention now. *"Allegedly* a bank robber. Innocent until proven guilty, right? You know something about him?"

"As it happens, yeah." He looked around to make sure nobody was listening to them. See, The Mask, well, he and I are like this." He held up his hand, realized he had one finger lifted, quickly added another digit. "We, ah, go way back. We went to college together."

"Are you serious?"

"Yeah, I went to college."

"No, I didn't mean that."

"You do want to see him, don't you?"

"Well, actually, I wouldn't mind. Why does he wear that mask?"

"It's terrible," Stanley said. "He never takes the mask off, never. It's kind of like part of him."

She shook her head.

He must be losing his mind, but even as he thought that, he couldn't just let her walk out of his life. "Look, I can get the word to him, if you want. How about meeting him tonight. Say, seven? In Peninsula Park? The muggers won't be out that early."

She hesitated, but only for a second. "Yeah. I'd

like that. I'll be there. Thanks, Stanley. You are such a—"

"Don't say it," he said. "I'm not as sweet as you think."

He watched her leave. Sighed and shook his head.

Stanley, Stanley. What *are* you doing?

Early in the afternoon with the majority of the worried customers finally cleared out, Stanley's phone rang. He picked it up, kept plugging away at his computer.

"Stanley?" A woman's voice.

"Yes?"

"Hi, it's Peggy."

"Why, hi. How are you?"

"Great. My landlord says if I don't come up with three months' rent by tomorrow, he's gonna throw me out. They are going to cancel 'Ask Peggy.' I still don't have squat on this Mask character."

"Sorry."

"Not your fault. But listen, I heard some scuttlebutt and I wanted to know if you'd heard anything about it."

"Scuttlebutt?"

"Yes. The word on the street is, the guy who owns the Coco Bongo Club—Dorian Tyrel?—he's offering fifty thousand dollars to whoever can deliver The Mask to him."

"Why would he want to do that?"

"He's a gangster, who knows why?"

"Why tell me?"

"Well, I am beginning to get the feeling you may know something."

"Excuse me?"

"Oh, I don't mean I think you're him, but you two seem to run in the same circles. I checked the records. He showed up at your brownstone, the garage where your car is, the bank where you work, and the club you got thrown out of the other night."

"I didn't get thrown out. They never let me in. How did you know that?"

"I have my sources. Anyway, what I was wondering was, do you know how to get in touch with this guy? I mean, if I could get an interview with him, the paper would give me a slot in an Edge City second."

"I wish I could help you, Peggy, but it's just a series of coincidences. I don't know the guy."

There was a long pause. "You're sure?"

He felt guilty. He'd told Tina he knew The Mask and here he was lying to Peggy, who was probably a lot nicer person and who really needed to know. "Well. Tell you what. If I run into him, I'll pass the word along."

"Thanks, Stanley. I really appreciate it. Let me make you dinner or something some night, okay?"

Stanley couldn't believe what he was hearing. Was Peggy asking him over to her place? No woman had ever done that—unless you counted his mother and his elderly sister, and they didn't count. They were relatives.

"Uh, I'd like that."

"Great. Keep in touch, Stanley. I'll look forward to hearing from you."

He cradled the phone. Looked a his computer and realized he'd been writing *All work and no play makes Stanley a dull boy* over and over again. He cleared the screen.

Maybe this whole business with The Mask wasn't so bad after all. He had two women who wanted to get next to him in his alter ego, both of them great looking and accomplished. When you got right down to it, what did it matter? It was the same guy who was going to wake up and have breakfast with her in the morning, no matter who she thought she was getting the night before, right?

Something to think about.

Dorian lit a cigarette and took a deep drag, despite the "No Smoking" sign in the Swede's reception room. The secretary, a red-haired beauty with dagger-pointed fake nails, frowned at him. Sitting to either side of Dorian were two of the Swede's bigger legbreakers, men who had to be six-six and three hundred pounds apiece, easy.

The secretary's intercom buzzed and she smiled at Dorian. "You can go in now, Mr. Tyrel."

Dorian looked around for a place to stub the butt, didn't see an ashtray.

The left-hand legbreaker, a man who looked like a shaved grizzly bear, stood. Dorian handed him the cigarette. "Here you go, Bluto. Present for you."

The giant smiled. Put the cigarette into his mouth and swallowed it.

Brrrr.

In the office, the Swede was practicing his golf swings. He had one of those holographic walls, a projected image of a real course with a special wall to catch the balls. It was just like being on the fairway at Pebble Beach or somewhere. The Swede set himself and swung, knocked the ball a good three hundred simulated yards, and dropped it fifty feet short of the green.

"Nice shot," Dorian said.

"It was, wasn't it? Par five, I'm on the green in two. Easy birdie." He turned and smiled. "Good of you to drop by, Dorian."

"You could have called. You didn't need to send Goliath and Atlas here for me."

The Swede pulled an iron from his back, set himself, chipped the ball. It flew, hit five feet on the other side of the pin, rolled back three feet. He switched the iron for a putter, clicked a switch, and the wall's image changed to show the putt. He stepped up, tapped it into the cup.

"I'm five strokes under and this is the eighth hole. If I par the ninth, I'll beat my old record. But if I bogey it, I'll only tie. I don't like wind chimes and I don't like to lose and I also don't like to break even, do you know what I mean, Dorian?"

"Yeah."

The Swede nodded to Goliath and Atlas. They grabbed Dorian as if he were a Ken doll and slammed him down onto the golf mat on the floor, faceup. Held him there as the Swede bent and put a yellow wooden tee into his mouth.

Dorian spat the tee out.

Atlas came out of his jacket with a .50 Desert Eagle, a gun that fired a bullet bigger than Dorian's thumb. Probably take your head clean off at close range with one shot. Dorian froze as the bore lined upon his left eye.

The Swede nodded and Goliath put another tee in Dorian's mouth.

Dorian left it there.

The Swede bent and put a ball on the tee. It wobbled a little as Dorian shoved it as high as he could with his tongue, holding the very tip of the bitter-tasting wood in his teeth. He couldn't believe this was happening, but he knew what the Swede was gonna do.

"If I bogey this next hole because of a bad tee shot, you go home by way of the express elevator, Dorian." He nodded at the window.

They were nineteen stories up. Although that didn't make a whole lot of difference, Dorian would be just as dead if they were on the fifth floor. Or the third.

The Swede set himself. Had to choke up on the wood a little because the ball was so high. Said, "The cops tried to shut the club down this morning. Said you were shooting up the place like a pink-slipped postal worker last night. I had to pull all kinds of strings to make the whole thing go away. I was embarrassed. I owe some favors now. I hate being embarrassed. I also hate owing favors, Dorian."

He touched the ball lightly, cocked the club . . .

Dorian closed his eyes and prayed to all the gods he could think of.

The club just brushed his lips but the rush of air was the loudest sound he'd ever heard.

"Look at that. On the green. A blind monkey could par from there. You are a lucky man, Dorian. And because we go way back, I'm going to cut you a little slack. You have a week to relocate. Another town would be good, another state better, and another planet best of all. After that, if I catch you in Edge City, I will break my new nine iron in on your skull, do you understand?"

The two legbreakers jerked Dorian to his feet. "Hold him still."

They did. The Swede bent and pulled the fiberglass knife from Dorian's sock. Twirled it in his hand expertly, turned, and threw it. It spun across the room and stuck up in the wall.

"One week, starting today, Dorian."

"Up yours," Dorian said. It was a lot braver than he felt. A little blood trickled down his chin from his slightly split lower lip.

The Swede chuckled. "You always did have more balls than brains. Escort Mr. Tyrel to the street, please."

As the two men frog-marched him through the lobby toward the elevators, Dorian realized he was going to have to go with what he had. Sweet and Orlando might not be too smart, but they were loyal. It only took one well-placed bullet to kill a man, even a man like the Swede. He was gonna have to see about making sure the bullet got where it was supposed to.

He had a week. That was gonna have to do.

11

The headline said, MASKED FREAK ROBS BANK: POLICE SCOUR CITY.

Stanley frowned as he shoved thirty-five cents into the coin slot and removed all of the papers in the rack. He looked around in a panic for a place to dump them.

Isn't going to help, Stanley. There are thousands of paper boxes in the city. You don't have enough money to clean them all out. Besides, what are you worried about? The guy in the picture doesn't look anything like you, now, does he?

He found a garbage basket and dropped the papers into it, but he didn't feel any better. It finally struck home: this was serious business.

He was a *bank robber*!

What was he going to do? It was all fine and good to want to impress Tina, but what was going to happen to him if the cops put two and two together, like Peggy had done? Things could get real bad.

Worse, he could be crazy, and all of this some kind of delusion: the nightmares, the headlines, everything. He could be so far around the bend as to be heading in the same direction again. And even if he wasn't, he was out of control, that was for sure. Stanley would never rob a bank. The Mask wouldn't think twice.

As he wandered down the hot sidewalk, tired, sticky, and too poor to take a cab—no way was he going to spend that stolen money—he passed in front of a bookstore. There in the window was a prominent display: *The Masks We Wear*, by Dr. Arthur Neuman.

It plucked a chord in Stanley. He'd heard about this guy somewhere, he couldn't remember where right off. An expert on masks, a shrink.

Maybe he could help.

Stanley looked at the wall of the office. There were dozens of masks there, tribal masks from Africa and South America, Victorian costume-ball half faces, ceramic ones from God knew where. Masks made from puffin feathers and beaks. Others from ivory, bone, even brass.

Neuman toyed with his cold pipe, looking somewhat uncomfortable. "I was just leaving, Mr. Ipkiss, and this is unusual, most unusual, no appointment—"

Stanley cut him off. "Look, this is an emergency and you're the only one who can help!" He felt his face twitch, as it had several times before.

Neuman sat up straighter behind his desk and look alarmed. "Mr. Ipkiss? Are you unwell?"

"I've got a date in a couple of hours with the girl of my dreams, doctor, only she doesn't know it's me she's meeting—"

"I hardly think a blind date qualifies as an emergency," Neuman began. "I mean, really—"

"No, you don't understand." He popped open his briefcase and carefully removed the mask. "Take a look at this."

Neuman looked a little more interested. He took the mask, turned it in his hands, examined it with the touch and skill of an expert. "Ah, very nice. Norse. Tenth, maybe eleventh century. See the runes, here? A fine piece of work. Do you want to sell it?"

"No."

"How did you come by it?" He continued to inspect the mask.

"I found it. Or it found me." Stanley reached out, grabbed the mask, snatched it away. "It doesn't matter. What matters is, it is ruining my life."

He lost control of his face again, felt it contort. Neuman was looking at the mask and missed it.

"I put it on, and I . . . change."

"You think the mask turns you into someone else?"

"On the nose, doctor."

.

"Mr. Ipkiss, please. This is nothing more than a piece of wood." He gestured at the mask. "Valuable wood, yes; historically significant, to be sure; but a carving, not some magical device."

"But your book—"

"—uses masks as a metaphor for our complex personalities. We are large, Mr. Ipkiss, we contain multitudes, as the poet says. To protect ourselves and suppress the id, we don facades to show to the rest of the world."

"This one works in reverse." Stanley waved the mask.

"Oh, really? Show me?"

Stanley took a deep breath. "All right. But you asked for it."

He pressed the mask into place. Started to spin, but slower than usual. "Whooaa!"

After a few seconds he stopped.

"Whooaa?"

Stanley felt like a complete idiot. He looked at the mask, pressed it back against his face again.

Nothing.

"It—it didn't work."

"And that really surprises you? Mr. Ipkiss—Stanley—the mask is nothing but a reflection—an extension—of you. The inner you."

Stanley was only half listening. He was thinking out loud. "It worked last night. And the night before. Maybe—maybe it only works at night. After dark. Or something." He looked at the doctor. "What kind of carvings did you say these were?"

"Scandinavian. It looks like the name for the Norse god of Mischief, Loki, I'd guess offhand. Such a troublemaker that Odin banished him from Valhalla, so they say."

"And into this mask, maybe," Stanley said, nodding to himself. That would explain a lot. In fact, magic was the only thing that would explain it. Not science fiction but fantasy. Yep—

"Stanley, I'm sorry, but I really do have to leave now. If you'd like to make an appointment for another time, I would be happy to take you on as a patient."

"But—but—what about my date?"

"Your date?"

"Yeah, do I go as myself or as him?" He waved the mask.

"If I tell you, do you promise to leave?"

Stanley nodded.

Neuman stood, shook his head, came around the desk. He put one fatherly arm around Stanley's shoulders. "Stanley. Go as yourself. Wear the mask or not, it won't matter. You're the same either way."

Stanley shook his head. The guy was full of it. He didn't have a clue, couldn't help. "You don't read the papers, do you, Dr. Neuman? Or watch much TV news."

He turned and walked out.

"Boss, I got a copy of the latest stuff in the cop file about The Mask," Orlando said.

Dorian sat at his desk, tapping in a new scenario

on his computer. How to Kill the Swede Without Getting Your Butt Shot Off? was the question of the day.

"Yeah, yeah, put it in that basket."

"I thought you was in a hurry for it."

Dorian looked away from the pixels dancing on the computer's monitor. "Well, I was. But that was then and this is now. Right at this moment I have more important things to worry about, don't you see?"

"Uh, sure, boss."

"Go and find Sweet. Then I want you two to look around and find some boys who can be trusted to shoot first and shut up later. Boys who aren't affiliated with the Swede."

"Huh?"

Dorian sighed. "Out-of-town muscle, Orlando. I want eight or ten shooters. Guys who can hit what they aim at would be nice, if you can find them. Call Chicago, Detroit, D.C., whoever. I need them here in three days, tops."

"We going to war or something?"

"That's exactly what we're going to do," Dorian said. "War. Now hustle your butt up."

Orlando left and Dorian leaned back in his chair. This was gonna be tricky no matter which way he went at it. The Swede was thick with protection and his boys had IQs higher than their bullet calibers, most of them. Even with a dozen decent shooters, a stand-up fight would be suicide. So that was out.

But—if he could get enough of a diversion

going, hit a few of the Swede's less-well-protected places of business, and get the man scrambling, then maybe. He was gonna have to be like a magician, he'd have to get the Swede watching one hand while the other hand did the dirty work. Four or five shooters throwing lead in a couple of places where the Swede's organization was vulnerable, that would get his attention.

'Course, the Swede would know who was behind it. Give him that. He didn't have any enemies he knew about walking around within danger range, he either hit them or, like he was doing to Dorian, banished them. So when it all started to come down, he'd go looking for the closest target first and that would be Dorian.

So he'd have to use that to his advantage, Dorian knew. He also knew how the Swede would react. Man takes a swing at you, he opens himself up for a counterpunch, Dorian had learned that from the Swedeman himself. But if you're expecting the counter, then you can throw a counter of your own. Punch, block, punch, block, punch! Or maybe a well-placed kick to the *cojones*. Whatever. The point was, he had to get the Swede thinking and moving in the wrong direction so he wouldn't see the real danger until it was too late.

Not easy, even though he knew what had to be done. Knowing *what* wasn't the same as knowing *how* and neither of them was the actual *doing* of it.

He leaned back toward the computer. He had all the information he needed, he was pretty sure of that, it was just a matter of dredging it up and putting it to the right use. The battle was won in the brain, Swede used to tell his boys. You have the right attitude, the right plan, and the fight is over before you put the gloves on.

Yeah.

They'd made a boxwood topiary that said, WELCOME TO LANDFILL PARK, right at the entrance. Below that, a little metal sign said, somewhat ironically, NO DUMPING.

Given that the entire park was a garbage dump overplanted with grass and fast-growing trees, the joke wasn't lost on native Edgians.

Stanley walked into the park. There was a nice, if somewhat fragrant breeze blowing, cooling the summer evening a little. He carried his briefcase and had removed his coat and tie. Not far inside the entrance, he saw Tina sitting on a park bench. There were a few couples strolling up and down the walks or lolling about on the lawns, but nobody close to Tina.

Stanley swallowed. She was beautiful in the evening sunshine. It wasn't close to dark yet, but a bank of clouds to the west dimmed the light some and the effect was striking.

He opened his briefcase. Took out the mask. Stared at it.

Tina checked her watch. Frowned. Looked up as she heard the confident voice: "Hiya, baby!"

Her smile faltered when she saw him. "Oh. Stanley. What are you doing here?"

His confidence melted like chocolate on a hot sidewalk. "Uh, I was, just, you know, kidding around. Thought I'd take a walk in the park on my way home. You know."

"Is your friend coming?"

"Oh, yeah. Probably got caught in traffic, but he'll be here."

"Great." She looked around. "I hardly ever come here. It's very nice. Hard to believe it used to be a garbage dump, isn't it?"

Stanley shifted his weight back and forth, dangled the case from hand to hand. "Yeah, it is. 'Cept for a little ripe smell now and then. Get terrific sunsets here. All those methane emissions or whatever really pick up the color. Get greens and blues sometimes."

"You come here a lot?"

"Not so much anymore. I used to."

Tina looked around.

"You really want to see this guy, don't you?"

"Well . . . yeah."

"How come—if you don't mind my asking? I mean, I know him and all, but he's kinda weird looking and passing strange."

She nodded. "That's true. But he has this . . . confidence. There's this element of . . . I don't know . . . danger about him."

Stanley nodded. Women who fall in love with serial killers. A common phenomenon. Lawyers,

judges, doctors, even the most intelligent and edu-
cated women were sometimes drawn to the dead-
liest of men. Oprah had done a show on it. Or
maybe it was Donahue?

Stanley said, "Yeah, well, I guess I'd better be
going. See you."

He started to walk away.

"Stanley?"

"Yeah?"

"I was thinking about what you said today.
Maybe you're right."

"I am? About what?"

"Believing in myself. Maybe if I did, I wouldn't
have to rely on somebody like Dorian so much."

"Dorian? Dorian Tyrel?"

"You know him? He's sort of my . . . manager."

"Tina, you need to be careful around him. He's
a criminal. A gangster."

"It's sweet of you to worry."

Stanley felt a sudden urge to scream at the
dreaded word. He contained himself. "No, I'm serious, Tina, he's dangerous."

"I can take care of myself. I always have."

"People around him tend to wind up dead."

"Listen, I do what I have to do to get by. I'm a
survivor."

"Yeah. Surviving with a thug, no faith in yourself, taking a free ride."

He didn't mean it to come out so bitter. He saw
from her expression he'd scored a painful hit.

"Listen, I'm sorry. It's none of my business. I gotta go."

He hurried away.

He heard her call out to him and he almost turned and went back, but *he* wasn't what she wanted.

And he knew how to give her what she *did* want.

The Mask bounded into the clearing and came down next to the bench as lightly as a balloon. Tina turned, saw him, and he swept her off her feet. A beret appeared on his head, he grew a pencil-thin gigolo mustache. While holding her stretched out and nearly on her back on the ground, he said, "*Ah, chérie! C'est moi! Jet'aime, Jet'aime*, Je any old tame! At last we are together, *mon petit bonbon*!"

If the French accent had been any more syrupy, he could bottle it for pancakes.

He was about to plant a big kiss on her when he heard something in the bushes. "Hold that thought," he said. He let her go, but she hung in the air as if suspended by wires. The Mask darted to his left in a blur, then stopped with tent peg- a stob-in-the-ground twang.

Well, well. Look who was hiding in the bushes.

Kellaway and two uniformed officers, watching.

"If it isn't the peeping O'Learys," The Mask said, grinning wider. "Now, boys, it isn't polite to sneak around spying on people, now is it?"

Kellaway pulled a com from his belt and said, "This is Kellaway! I need backup now! Scramble the

SWAT team, every available man, Landfill Park now!''

The Mask turned, blurred back to where he'd left Tina hanging. Resumed his previous position, stood her up. "Ah, Tina, our love is like a rose . . .'' He dropped into an imitation of Groucho. Waggled his cigar, said, ". . . and I'm feeling pretty thorny myself!''

Tina blinked.

The Mask lost Groucho and stood upright. "Care for a cigarette, my dear? I usually wait until after, but we're going to have company soon.''

His hands blurred toward her face and suddenly she had a dozen cigarettes in her mouth. "Regular? Menthol? Filter? Slims? Tiparillo? Here, let me get that for you. . . .''

He produced a blowtorch from his pocket with one hand and grabbed all the cigarettes from Tina's perfect mouth with the other hand. Stuck them into his own lips and flashed the torch over the ends. Took a giant inhalation and smoked them all to ash with one breath. He exhaled a huge cloud of smoke which formed a heart shape. Another puff, and an arrow of smoke pierced the heart.

"Ah, well, let's move on to *amore*, eh?''

He tossed the torch aside and lunged at Tina, arms outspread.

"Freeze, Mask!''

He did just that, a foot off the ground, looking like a photograph.

Sunday in the park with The Mask.

Kellaway and the uniforms, guns drawn, approached carefully.

"Put your hands up!"

The Mask said, through stiff lips, "Vut you told ve to freeze."

Kellaway grabbed his gun with both hands, came around to stand directly in front of The Mask.

"Stand back, miss. This psycho is dangerous. Okay, unfreeze! You're under arrest!"

The Mask dropped to the ground, fell to his knees, clasped his hands together as if in prayer. "Under arrest? No, no, it wasn't me? I'm innocent, I tell you! I was framed! It was the one-armed man! Deep Throat in the garage! The butler!"

He lifted an eyebrow at the lieutenant.

"Not buying it, eh? Okay, copper, I confess, don't use the rubber hoses! I did it. I was young, foolish, so full of life, but I made a mistake and now I'm ready to pay my debt to society!"

He started crying. Water gushed from his eyes like taps had been turned on, splashed on the ground. Formed a salty puddle.

Kellaway backed away from the rapidly spreading puddle.

"Wh-what'll they do with me, officer? Am I going to the Big House? Will I get the chair? The rope? The needle? Will I be bunking with Bubba?"

"That's up to a judge, pal. Search him."

One of the uniforms moved in. He started rummaging in the zoot suit's pockets. He came up with a comb, a package of vitamins. A sousaphone. A bazooka. He dropped them on the ground, fished in the same pocket. Came out with a picture.

"Hmm. Looks like your wife, Lieutenant," the cop said.

"Gimme that." Kellaway grabbed the picture. It *was* his wife. There was a note clipped to the photo: *Call me, lover, let's do it again!* The number was Kellaway's home phone.

"You rotten little—"

He lunged, but the other uniform held him back.

"Jeez, I thought you had a sense of humor," The Mask said. "I mean, *you* married her, didn't you?"

Kellaway struggled. "Bastard!"

To the cop holding him, The Mask said, "Here, sonny, you missed this." He pulled an anvil out of his pocket and handed it to the cop, who took it before his brain kicked in. The weight of the anvil jerked him to the ground.

The Mask pulled a fencing foil and whipped it back and forth at Kellaway, making the sign of Zorro on his pants. "*Adios, amigos!* Underwear! Underwear!" His body shot off, leaving his head on a stretched neck for a beat before it followed with a sound like a giant sheet of canvas being torn: *Jjjjrrr riiiippp!*

The Mask arrived at a twelve-foot-high stone wall with a big wooden gate. He zipped through the gate, slammed it behind him. Threw a huge bolt, pulled a giant padlock from his pocket, and snapped it into place, slammed down a steel plate, zipped up a giant zipper, then hammered in dozens of nails at eye-smiting speed with an oversized hammer. Then he sagged against the gate and breathed rapidly.

"Whew!"

He turned around. His eyes bugged out, snapped back into place.

There were dozens, scores, *hundreds* of cops arriving. Cars, helicopters, SWAT vans, motorcycles, bicycles, all full of cops.

"PUT YOUR HANDS OVER YOUR HEAD AND DON'T MOVE OR WE'LL SHOOT!"

"You talkin' to me? You talkin' to *me*?"

Dozens of cops cocked their weapons. It sounded like a herd of demented crickets going into heat.

The Mask gave the cops a big grin. Whispered an aside to nobody:

"Uh . . . oh . . . I got a bad feeling about this."

12

The cavalry wasn't coming. Neither were the Lone Ranger, Roy Rogers, or Lash Larue. It was just him and all these guys with all them guns.

Only one thing to do, The Mask realized. "All right, boys, hit it!"

There came a drummer's rimshot, and a huge spotlight flared to limn The Mask. He wore a straw boater and carried a cane. He spun the cane around his wrist, put the tip of it down, grabbed it with both hands, and struck a dramatic pose.

Rumba music began to play, the sound coming from the police radios, passersby with ghetto blasters, and every car stereo in the city.

Ah, the rumba!

A startled female cop stepped forward like a puppet on strings, took off her hat, and shook out her long hair. Began to sing to the beat.

The Mask smiled at her, gave her a nod.

She looked horrified but continued the song. It was peppy, up-tempo, the perfect kinda thing for a hot summer day. He listened as she ran through the open lyrics. Nice voice, for a cop.

She swept one arm out toward the Mask and he tilted the boater down, took a step forward, moving his hips to the rumba rhythm. Looked at the crowd with a sly gleam in his eyes as he picked up the tune in a voice redolent with island salsa.

Oh, he had them now!

A young cop who'd no doubt cut his teeth on a television and black-and-white reruns said, "Hey, he sounds just like whatshisname, you know, Lucy's husband. Babaloo?"

One of the older Latino cops shook his head. "He should. That's the 'Cuban Pete Rumba,' one of the songs Desi Arnaz used to sing, God rest him."

The Mask leaped up and hooked a lamppost with his cane, spun around it in a slow spiral. He slid, did several complicated dance steps, winked, nodded, waved his hat at the audience. Now the area in front of the gate had morphed into a stage, and he danced near the footlights.

Kellaway and his two uniforms came around the end of the wall, which was ornamental and extended only a few yards in either direction past the gate.

"Sweet Jaysus," one of the uniforms said.

"Shut up," Kellaway said.

"He's not bad, though," the other uniform ventured.

"You shut up, too."

The Mask grinned. He could hear every word the startled cops said and it was very amusing. But back to business. A performer couldn't let his mind wander when he was onstage, could he?

He leaped over the footlights and into the street, danced toward the heavily armed cops, stopped just short of the astonished front rank of the thin blue line. Twirled until his legs were twisted together like a plane's rubber-band motor, then spun back and lifted a few feet into the air before floating down.

He did a few quick steps and broke into the saucy chorus. Ah, yes! Black beans and yellow rice, good cigars, and alllll that sugarcane! And don't forget the rum.

He waved at the cops. The front line shuffled forward, faces full of surprise and fear as they formed a chorus line and began to high-step and kick to the music.

The Mask grinned. Ah, Busby Berkeley would be so proud!

Behind him, Kellaway said, "Goddammit!"

The SWAT team went into a complicated interweave, forming a flower whose petals opened and closed. A huge swimming pool formed and began to shimmer and sparkle in the background.

Ah, where *was* Esther Williams when you needed her?

The Mask rumba-ed up to the female cop who'd started the number. They did a half rumba, half tango across the street, hips glued together. They sang in perfect two-part harmony. She really *did* have a good voice.

He dipped the officer, who instead of her uniform now wore a white peasant off-the-shoulder blouse and a bright print skirt and sandals—though she still had her weapons strapped on over her new clothes.

"Come on, everybody! Rumba!" The Mask yelled.

The two uniforms with Kellaway started to gyrate to the music.

"You go out there and I'll shoot you both," Kellaway said.

The uniforms shrugged helplessly and rumba-ed away.

Kellaway cursed loudly and started for a nearby squad car. He found the keys, opened the trunk, came out with a tear-gas gun. Slid a shell into the chamber.

The entire crowd of police was dancing now. Pedestrians came to see what the commotion was about joined in. They formed a conga line.

Dum dum dum dum dum dump*!*

Kellaway fired the tear-gas gun into the air. The shell arced high, fell, and exploded ten feet above the ground. The cloud spewed and enveloped the dancers. They began to cough and rub at their eyes.

The spell was broken.

Aw, too bad.

The Mask froze in midstep and looked at Kella-way. Waggled his eyebrows, pushed his boater back on his head with the tip of his cane.

"Arrest that *thing*!" Kellaway yelled.

Cops went for their weapons again.

An impossibly long vaudeville hook shot out of nowhere and snagged The Mask's neck.

"Oops, that's showbiz, folks!"

The hook snatched The Mask away so fast his hat and cane were left floating in the air.

With Kellaway yelling behind him, The Mask darted into the coughing crowd. The tear-gas mist was still thick enough to provide some cover.

The Mask made it to the other side of the park. Lost 'em. Keystone koppers, what a buncha rubes. A buncha maroons—

He nearly ran into an old lady, who screamed at his appearance.

"Hey, you're no prize either, Granny!"

She turned and ran away as fast as she could. Pretty quick for an old gal.

But maybe it was time to ring the curtain down on this number.

He grabbed at the mask and pulled.

It stretched like taffy. It *screamed*, a high-pitched wail, as it popped clear of his face with a cow-pull-ing-her-foot-from-the-mud *swock*. Did *not* want to come off.

Stanley found himself alone. He jammed the mask under his shirt and into his pants.

He tried to go back to blend in with the crowd of pedestrians drawn to the fray.

Kellaway arrived and spotted him. "Hold it right there, Ipkiss! Move and you're Swiss cheese!"

Uh-oh. The jig was up. Kellaway knew he was The Mask.

Well. So much for his life.

Stanley ran. They wouldn't shoot with all these people around. He headed across the street, dodged between the gridlocked cars.

A bullet *spanged* the brick wall of the building next to Stanley's head.

He yelled back at Kellaway. "Are you crazy! You might hit an innocent bystander!"

He ducked into an alley, prayed it wasn't a dead end.

More bullets zipped past, splashed against the walls and Dumpsters. He didn't hear the shots until after the rounds hit. Probably wouldn't hear the one that killed him. Jeez!

He ran into the street at the end of the alley. They were gonna catch him. He was going to have to put the mask back on to get away—

A car pulled up, burned rubber in a panic stop. "Stanley! Get in!"

It was Peggy Brandt.

It was a beat-up jalopy, but it was faster than he was on foot. He jerked the door open and leaped in.

She burned more rubber as she stomped the gas.

By the time the cops reached the street, the car was a hundred yards away and gaining.

Stanley looked at her. "Where are we going?"

"Somewhere safe."

She didn't say much on the ride.

Neither did he.

Stanley cupped his hands around a mug of coffee. They were in the printing-and-shipping warehouse of Peggy's newspaper. Around them, bound stacks of tomorrow's early edition stood piled chest-high. In the background, the hum and clack of automatic machinery grumbled as it folded and banded more papers. The presses were stopped, but it was still fairly noisy.

If he looked as bad as he felt, Stanley would scare away a hungry werewolf.

Peggy sat next to him, sipping at coffee of her own.

"So, what *is* happening to you, Stanley? I saw that thing turn into you. You're lucky I was there."

He shook his head. "Thanks. I dunno. It's crazy. Whenever I put this on"— he held up the mask—"I can do anything, *be* anything, but I'm paying for it. It's ruined my life—what life I had. The cops are after me. I'm probably going to do twenty years in the state pen. My father was right, I can't do anything without screwing up. I'm a total failure."

"Hey, you do a mean rumba."

He glared at her.

She shook her head. "Listen, Stanley, I don't know about all this stuff, but I do know that the letter you sent to my column was from a guy with more guts and heart than most of the creeps I've met in this town. Whatever this mask is, you don't need it. You're already all you ever need to be. You're a worthwhile person on your own."

He blinked and looked at her. "Wow. You really mean that?"

She paused. "Well, actually . . . no. I just wanted to keep you talking."

"Huh?"

"Move and you die," a man's voice said.

Stanley turned. Saw Dorian Tyrel and two thugs standing there. All three had guns pointed right at him.

"What took you so long?" Peggy said. "I've been vamping forever here."

"This is the guy? Are you serious? This dweeb?" To Stanley, he said, "You look familiar? Do I know you?"

"No. I don't think so."

"I'm good with faces. Yours is familiar. It'll come to me later."

Peggy said, "I don't want to interrupt old home week or anything, but do you have the fifty thou?"

"Yeah." He hefted a briefcase. Set the case on the floor.

Peggy nodded. "This is him. When he puts that mask on, he turns into the green guy."

Stanley stared at her, stunned. "Peggy!?"

"Sorry, Stanley, but I couldn't lose my condo. You know how hard it is to find a decent apartment in this town? Nothing personal, I do think you're a nice guy, but business is business."

"Sweet."

One of the thugs grabbed the mask and handed it to Dorian.

Then both thugs grabbed Stanley. Marched him to where a giant paper shredder was doing its work. Held him butt first over the machine's maw.

Dorian said, "Okay, pal. Where is my money?"

"It—it's at my apartment! In the closet!"

Dorian nodded at the thugs. "Ah, well. Looks like you're about to get a little behind in your work." They started to hoist him into the machine.

"Hey, you said you weren't going to hurt him!" Peggy said.

Dorian looked at her. Shrugged. "Okay. He's a worm, I can step on him anytime. Besides, I need to make sure he isn't lying about my money. That bank job was worth more than a million, you know." He looked at his boys. Waved them away from the shredder with a jerk of his head. They set Stanley back on his feet.

"So, how does this thing work?" He held up the mask.

"I don't know. You just put it on and it does."

"Yeah?"

The one called Sweet said, "Careful boss."

"Teach your grandma to suck eggs," Dorian said. He grinned.

Raised the mask . . .

There came a clap of thunder. A whirlwind of

fire and multicolored light surrounded Dorian, red, green, blue, and the force of it nearly knocked Stanley over, it was like staring into the face of a hurricane. Papers flew, the bodyguards had to lean into the wind. Peggy was blown backward five feet, as if she were on ice skates.

The wind died, the flashing lights faded.

Dorian was . . . changed.

Stanley stared at the apparition. Whereas the mask had turned him into a zoot-suiter of cartoonish proportions, a cross between a frog and a goblin, Dorian had an entirely different look. He was like some kind of evil genie, fresh from a thousand years imprisoned in a bottle and pissed about it. He was bigger, meaner looking, and the neuvo-gangster appearance was still evident—the earring he wore had become the size of a marble—but his grin was more like that of a psychopathic T-rex. His eyes glowed a malevolent green, the infernal light shining forth like LEDs, and when he spoke, his voice was a powerful bass rumble:

"What a rush!"

Sweet said, "Whoa, boss! You okay in there?"

"Better than okay, idiot. I feel great!" He sounded like Tony the Tiger run through a thousand-watt amplifier into speakers nine feet tall. The force of it knocked all four of the watchers down.

Stanley got to his feet, watched Peggy do the same.

Sweet said, "Check it out, Orlando, the boss is *bad*!"

Peggy moved to the briefcase Dorian had brought into the place, picked it up. "Well, I'll just be taking my money and running along, if you don't mind. Make yourselves at home. *Mi casa es su casa.*"

Dorian slid across the floor without moving his feet, came to a stop in front of Peggy. "Must you? We could make beautiful music together."

Ravel's *Boléro* began playing in the background.

"I don't think so. That wasn't part of the deal." She turned slightly to go around him.

The music changed to "Ride of the Valk'ries."

"Oh? Come on, how many chances are you going to get to go one-on-one with a man like me?"

"I'll pass."

"Ah, I see. Only want what's coming to you, is that it?"

"Hold it a second," she said. She put down the briefcase, opened her purse, pulled out a snub-nose .38. Pointed it at Dorian. "Like I said, freakazoid, I'll be running along."

Dorian's impossible shark's grin got wider. "Hey, a Ladysmith. Nice piece."

The grotesque raised his hands. Behind them, the presses cranked up and began running papers, zipping them along on the automatic conveyer.

The music changed to the old Alfred Hitchcock TV-show theme.

"Funeral March of a Marionette," Stanley believed it was.

Uh-oh . . .

Dorian/Mask spun, knocked the little revolver from Peggy's grip, grabbed her, and held her over his head like a bodybuilder with a barbell. "Girl like you deserves to have her face plastered all over page one, Peggy-O!"

Stanley yelled and lunged, but too late. Dorian/Mask threw the startled woman. She screamed as she flew, fell onto the conveyor, and was sucked into the giant press.

"Jesus!" somebody said. Sweet or Orlando.

"Run grab me a paper there, would you, Sweet?"

The thug hurried to obey.

He returned from where the press spat papers into a sorting machine. Came back, looking ashen.

"Gimme."

He tendered the paper.

Dorian/Mask laughed. "Check it out, little man."

He held the paper up. The headlines were bloodred. Said, REPORTER KILLED IN FREAK ACCIDENT. Under them, a picture of Peggy, screaming.

Stanley wanted to throw up.

Dorian/Mask turned to look at Stanley. "What are you looking so down about, chum? She sold you out." He grabbed the briefcase and opened it, showed it to Stanley. It was full of old phone books. "And cheap, too." He tossed the case aside.

"Wh-what'll we do with this guy, boss?" That from Orlando.

"Bring him along. The cops want The Mask,

we'll give the cops The Mask. What's left of him. Enough to ID by prints or dental records or something. Oh, and round up some of the new recruits. We're going to pay a little visit to a charity ball. Have a little chat with the Swede." He started to laugh, a booming noise that would put the finale of the 1812 Overture to shame.

Sweet and Orlando nervously joined in the laughter.

Stanley convulsed and almost lost his most recent meal. Yeah, she'd betrayed him, but surely even somebody like Peggy deserved better than to be the butt of a sick and killing joke. It wasn't for the money, they might have eventually gotten together.

Well. It looked as if they might be getting together soon anyway.

Still, it was disappointing. Peggy looked like the kind of girl you took home and introduced to your parents. Well, she had looked like that. And Tina, well, she didn't look like the kind of woman you wanted your mother or your Sunday-school teacher to know you even knew, much less brought home. But even so, there was something there. He didn't think she'd have sold him out.

Not that he had any particular reason to believe that, it was just a feeling.

Of course, he'd been wrong before.

Look where he was now.

He shook his head. It's always something, isn't it?

13

"Stay in the car," Dorian/Mask said to Sweet and Orlando. "I think I can handle old Stanley here by myself."

He grinned and felt the power of the mask flowing through him like a high-voltage charge. This was something. With this, he could do anything. Hell, he didn't even need the money this wimp had stashed upstairs in his apartment, he could knock down any bank wall in the country and clean it out, talk about juice! But it was the principle of the thing. Give little losers like this an inch and they'd go for the mile. Attention must be paid. Examples must be made. Sing a happy little serenade. . . .

Whoa. Better cool it, man. "Shall we?" he said to the wimp.

The little man nodded. Looked like crap, had dried puke on the front of his shirt, but he was

gonna look worse before he looked better. Teach
him to mess with Dorian Tyrel. The Man now, for
sure.

Inside the building, the elevator was broken. No
problemo. Dorian/Mask stepped in, shoved Stanley
ahead of him, and waved his hand. "Floor?"

"S-seven."

"You heard the man."

"Seventh floor! Hardware, auto parts, ladies underwear, and bank loot!" the elevator said.

They stepped out into the hall. "Which one?"

"There."

Dorian/Mask held Stanley's arm firmly and
urged him down the hall.

They were almost there when the apartment
door next to it opened and a woman in curlers with
a face that would stop a shockproof Timex stood
there. She held a double-barreled 12-gauge.

"Ipkiss! Is this monster a friend of yours?"

"No, Mrs. Peenman. I'm being held prisoner."

"Well, it probably serves you right. Hang
around with trash and see what it gets you? You—"
She waved the gun at Dorian/Mask. "Let him go.
He owes me rent. After he pays, you can have him
back."

"That didn't do any good last time, Mrs. Peenman," Stanley said. "And he's worse now than he
was."

Dorian/Mask took a deep breath and concen-
trated. There was a blur of energy around him, and
when it settled down, he wore blue tights, had a red

cape, and a big red *D* on his chest. He put his hands on his hips.

"Go ahead, Mama. Take your best shot."

The old battle-ax didn't hesitate. She unloaded both barrels. The recoil rocked her back on her heels.

Nasty one, wasn't she?

The gun spat flame just like she said it would. It hit Dorian/Mask's chest and splashed off in all directions.

Some of it washed back at the old bag. She screamed.

When the smoke cleared, she looked like a cartoon figure, all black and sooty, her hair singed off, the whites of her eyes huge in her scorched face.

Dorian/Mask laughed. "Is that it? That all you got? Sheeit. I spit harder than that." To prove it, he turned his head to the side and hawked. The glob flew, hit the floor, and blew a crater all the way through the ceilings and floors of the sixth story, the fifth, the fourth, and the third.

Dorian/Mask leaned over and looked into the hole. "Hmm. Must be getting weak in my old age. Should have gone right through to the basement."

The blackened woman screamed and slammed the door.

Dorian/Mask chuckled. "Reminds me, I want to get some Cajun food for supper. Now, where were we, hmm?"

In his apartment, Stanley opened the closet. Money cascaded out and swirled around his feet.

"Ah, there it is."

A dog whined behind them. Dorian/Mask turned. "A pooch. Hey, I like dogs. C'mere, pup."

The dog whined again and ran under the bed. He heard it coughing, trying to growl. He laughed. Pulled his wallet out of his pocket, waved his hand. All of the money flew into the air, stacked itself like a thick deck of cards, compressed, and fell into his hand in a packet thin enough to fit neatly in his wallet.

Dorian/Mask smiled and tucked the money away. "There we are, all safe and sound. Let's go, chump."

Stanley knew he was going to die. Probably Mrs. Peenman had called the cops and they'd be on their way, but if they messed with this mask wearer, he'd cream them. And unlike Stanley when he was The Mask, he wouldn't be joking around. This guy was a killer; if Stanley didn't get fried in the battle or shot by the cops, the gangster was going to finish him off as soon as he got around to it anyway. And there was nothing he could do about it. He was doomed.

As they left his apartment Stanley reached out automatically to close the door.

"Leave it," Dorian/Mask said. "You won't be coming back. We wouldn't want your little dog to be trapped in there, would we?"

As they walked down the hall Stanley glanced back. Sure enough, Milo poked his head out and watched them. Well. Maybe somebody would find him and take care of him. He was a pretty smart dog. He could catch a Frisbee and fetch keys. He could go downstairs, though he got winded pretty much trying to climb them. Maybe he'd be okay.

For sure, he was going to be better off than Stanley.

Dorian/Mask felt so good he decided he wasn't going to kill Ipkiss after all. Nah, not when he could be useful.

He looked at the little man crouched over against the Cad's back door. "Stanley, my boy, I've decided to let you keep on breathing for a while. Here's the deal—I give you to the cops and you take the fall. Otherwise . . ." He dragged his finger across his throat, went, "*Skiiik!*"

"Uh," Ipkiss began.

"Stanley, Stanley, which part of it didn't you understand? They are already looking for you—I have my sources at the department—and with you in hand, I'll be able to play for a time without anybody looking over my shoulder, *comprendo*? Not that it really matters, me being bulletproof and all, but there's a score I want to settle before I have to worry about combing cops out of my hair. Is it a deal?"

He flashed his great white shark's grin.

"I don't have much choice, do I?"

"Not any options *I'd* care to take, I was in your shoes." He held one foot up. It had Stanley's shoe on it. "Ugly footwear, my man." The shoe morphed back into his Italian loafer with the gold antique coin. "That's better."

"Okay. It's a deal."

"Good, good. Take us to the precinct, Sweet."

They drove in silence for a minute. Then Dorian/Mask discovered another great power he didn't know he had. "Hey, check this out."

He waved his hand and the back of the front seat turned into a giant-screen TV. "Lookie here, Stanley boy. It's our old friend Lieutenant Kellaway. Let's listen in, shall we? Turn up the sound, just so. . . ."

The image on the screen was of Kellaway and two other plainclothes cops standing outside the precinct near the front steps, talking. The camera zoomed in for a two-shot of Kellaway and one of the other detectives.

"I can't believe it," Kellaway said. "Cops so tough you could bounce bricks off 'em dancing in the streets like chorus girls. All over the damned ten o'clock news."

"Yeah, I hear the SWAT team got an offer to open for Wayne Newton in Vegas."

"I'm glad you think this is funny, Doyle. The captain is going to have my ass and badge for breakfast, maybe my pension thrown in for seasoning."

Dorian/Mask laughed. The car rocked on its shocks.

"Easy, boss, you want to wreck us?"

"Oh, but this is too good! Kellaway is suffering. I *told* him he'd be sorry. And I plan to get back to

him after I deal with the Swede, but first, I'll give
him a little gift. Let him think he's winning."

Onscreen, Doyle said, "C'mon, Kell, it wasn't
your fault. Something will turn up."

The shark face flashed an evil smile. "Stanley,
ask me what the most important thing about comedy is."

"Huh?"

"Go on, ask."

"Uh, what's the most important thing about—"

"Timing!" Dorian/Mask broke in. "Step on it,
Sweet!"

Onscreen, Kellaway said, "Forget it. I'm history.
The only thing that would save me is for Ipkiss to
fall into my lap—"

The Cad screeched around the corner. The cops
turned to look at it just as Dorian/Mask opened the
door and shoved Stanley out at speed.

He flew through the air and hit Kellaway,
knocked him down.

When the lieutenant sat up, Ipkiss was sitting on
his lap.

The Cad sped away.

"I'll be damned," Kellaway said.

"Uh, hi, Lieutenant."

Doyle grabbed him and put his hands behind
his back. Cuffed him.

"Uh, listen, I know what you're thinking—"

Kellaway grinned like a demented baboon.
Pulled a green rubber mask from Stanley's pocket.

Waved it under Stanley's nose. "I'm thinking maybe all my bad karma musta earned out. Let's go inside and have a chat, hey, Stanley?"

The cell wasn't so bad, Stanley thought. Not much worse than his apartment, when you got right down to it. It had a toilet and sink, a cot, even a barred window that looked out onto an alley full of Dumpsters. 'Course, it was filthy and graffiti covered the walls, but with a little work, he could clean it up. At least he was alive.

The guard locked the door. Said, "If you need anything, why, just dial room service." He jangled his key ring and walked away, chuckling. Went to the end of the corridor and turned on a tiny TV set on a table there, slouched into a chair.

Stanley sat on the cot. The hour he'd spent with Kellaway had been bad, but when he'd refused to talk, he knew they'd get tired sooner or later. They didn't need him to admit anything, anyway. They had the mask—not the *real* mask, of course—his fingerprints at the bank, and a whole lot of circumstantial evidence. Enough to hang him. He'd argued that since he worked at the bank, naturally they'd find his prints there, but it was kind of lame.

A dog barked in the alley. Stanley recognized the voice.

"Milo?"

He stood on the cot, peered out the barred window. Yep, there he was, next to a big mound of trash and boxes that overflowed the piled-high Dumpster.

The dog saw him, gave a happy *yip*.

Stanley shook his head. Now there was somebody he could trust. "Milo! Good boy! But you better forget about me, buddy. By the time I get out of here, your great-grandchildren will be old. Sorry."

Milo barked again, wagged his tail. Then turned and started to root through the trash. Came up with a chicken bone and began to gnaw on it.

"Hey, chicken bones are bad for you!"

Milo ignored him.

Stanley climbed down, sat on the cot. Stared at the wall. Fell asleep.

It was early the next morning when the guard appeared. "You got a visitor, Ipkiss."

"Huh?"

"C'mon. And don't do anything stupid."

He led Stanley to a small visitor's room. On the other side of a thick sheet of Plexiglas splitting a table down the middle was . . . Tina.

"Hi," he said. He sat at the table.

"It is true?" she asked. "Were you The Mask?"

"Well, yes. I was. But don't spread it around. A good lawyer might be able to cut a deal and get me out of here in ninety or a hundred years."

"Dorian has it now," she said. "The mask. He's turned into a monster."

"Big stretch there," he said.

"He's going to the charity ball tonight," she said. "And he's going to do something horrible."

"What—the lambada?"

"Not funny, Stanley. He's not like you were when you had it on. This is serious. I think he's going to hurt a lot of people."

Stanley nodded. "Yeah. I think the mask magnifies who you are. Me, I'm a repressed cartoon junkie and a romantic. It turned me into a funny wild man. Dorian . . . well, if I were you, I'd get out of town."

"I hear that. Thanks, Stanley."

"What for?"

"For treating me like a person instead of a party favor. For being a romantic, even a hopeless one."

"Hopeless. You got that right."

"I enjoyed our meeting in the park, you know."

"That wasn't the real me—"

"No," she cut in. "I mean before you put on the mask. When you *were* the real you."

He blinked. The last time a woman had complimented him, she'd sold him to a killer. But there wasn't anything Tina could do to him now, and besides, he believed her. He wanted to believe her.

She put her hand on the clear barrier. He mirrored her gesture.

"I *am* going to disappear for a while," she said. "But as soon as I get settled, I'll let you know where, okay?"

"Time's up," the guard said from the doorway.

"Listen, Stanley, I'll do what I can to help you.

You're an okay guy. I mean that. You take care of yourself."

She left. The guard took him back to his cell.

A minute or two later, not long, he heard screaming from the alley, then barking. He jumped up onto the cot and looked out.

Sweet and Orlando chased Tina into the alley. Milo ran around in circles, barking at them.

No! They were after Tina!

Stanley ran to the cell door and started hollering. "Guard! There's a woman being kidnapped in the alley! Guard!"

"Hey, shut up!" a prisoner down the hall yelled.

The guard sat at the end of the corridor, watching *Jeopardy* on his little television set. He ignored Stanley and turned the sound up:

"What is the U.S. Navy, Alex?"

"That's right!"

"Guard!"

But he was wasting his time.

Dorian/Mask had decided he was never going to take this thing off. He hadn't had to sleep or eat or even pee since he'd put it on and he felt like a billion dollars.

Sweet and Orlando approached the Cad where it was parked, blocking the alley behind the jail. They had Tina. They shoved her into the backseat with him.

"Well, well," he said. "Having a nice little chat with the cops, were we?"

"No. I was visiting Stanley."

"Oooh, how sweet. You and Ipkiss. Maybe you helped him beat us to that bank job, hey?"

"C'mon, Dorian, you know better than that. I wouldn't cross you."

Sweet returned and tapped on the Caddy's rear window. Dorian/Mask waved his hand and the window vanished.

"Found these in her car," Sweet said. He hefted two suitcases.

"Why, Tina, were you going to take a trip without telling your hot-lipped lover?"

"No—"

He grabbed her by the throat with one hand. The hand turned hairy, grew green claws. "You know what happened to the last bitch who tried to run out on me?"

"N-n-no!"

"Neither does anybody else, sugar." To Orlando, he said, "Let's go. We're all going to the ball and we want Cinderella here to get her gown, don't we?"

The smile was evil personified and it felt like a month of orgasms rolled into one. Yessir, yessir, this was the *only* way to fly!

He was having himself a fine time. Really fine. And it could only get better.

14

Stanley had never felt so helpless. The woman he loved was in danger and he couldn't do a thing about it!

Well, okay, yes, he had to admit it. He loved her. Even though she was beyond him, even though it would never be returned. How he felt was how he felt. No help for it.

Think, Stanley, *think*!

He paced the small cell. The sound of the guard's TV permeated the air. The theme music for final *Jeopardy*. Dah, dah, dah, dah, dah dah dah, dah, dah, dah, dah, *dah*, dah, dah-dah-dah-dah . . .

He went to the front of the cell and looked out. Down the corridor, the guard was eating a ham-and-cheese sandwich; Stanley could see and smell it. Looked as if he were about to fall asleep doing it, too.

There was nobody in the cells on either side of his, Stanley noticed. Either business was bad or they didn't want anybody to get too close to him. Understandable, given The Mask's behavior. If he could still do what The Mask had been able to do, they ought to figure the jail couldn't hold him.

Maybe they didn't want him to hurt any of the other felons when he blew the cell apart. Who knew what they thought?

He moved back into his cell, toward the window. He climbed onto the cot and stared through the narrow bars. No way he could squeeze through there, not in a million years. Not even a skinny six-year-old could make it.

Below, the alley was empty, save for the mounds of trash, grown even higher since yesterday. The effluvia of civilization almost reached the window, where it had been piled high on the Dumpster.

As he watched, Milo trotted back into view. Saw Stanley and woofed at him, tail wagging.

If it had been a cartoon, a lightbulb would have gone off over Stanley's head.

An idea!

In the back of the Cad, Dorian/Mask waved his hand and the seat in front of him blossomed into a TV screen again.

There stood Ipkiss on his cot in his cell, staring forlornly out through the bars of the small window.

"Aw, look, isn't he sad? Sooooo sad."

Tina glared at him.

"Oh, well. Enough of *Masterpiece Theatre*." He waved his hand and the image changed into that of a porno movie.

"Isn't this a lot more interesting? My, look at that."

Her eyes went wide.

He laughed. Oh, yeah, he was The Man, all right. In evvvveeeery sense of the word . . .

"Milo!"

The dog looked up at Stanley, wagged his tail.

"Come here, Milo. Come on, boy, come see me."

The dog ran back and forth in front of the heaped trash.

"Come on, you can do it. Climb up. Here, boy. Come on."

Milo looked a little puzzled but, after a moment, began to scrabble his way up the hillocks of garbage. He made it to a plateau in the Dumpster, where a piece of flattened corrugated cardboard box lay. Wagged his tail and yipped at Stanley.

"Good boy! Good puppy! But you have a way to go. Come on, Milo."

The dog looked around for a way up. Found a big juice can, hopped on it, managed to scramble higher as the juice can tumbled to cobblestones of the alley floor.

Eventually he worked his way to within a couple of feet of the window.

"Good dog! Now jump! I'll catch you."

Milo looked doubtful. Whined.

"Come on, you can do it. I have faith in you."

Milo jumped. Was six inches short. He dropped back and hit the top of the piled trash, nearly fell off.

"Easy, boy, easy! Come on. You can do it."

The little dog gathered himself again. Sprang. Almost.

He whined again.

"Come on, Milo. You're my only hope. Tina needs us!"

The little dog wheezed. Coughed. Drew himself together.

Leaped . . .

Stanley reached out and caught Milo's forelegs and pulled him in through the bars. "Gotcha! Good *boy*!"

After the dog finished licking his face, Stanley put him on the cot. "Stay."

Milo sat.

Stanley casually walked to the front of the cell and peeped out. The guard's TV was still blasting, but the guard was dozing in his chair.

Perfect.

Stanley returned to where Milo waited, tail going like a windshield wiper on high. Picked him up. "Okay, Milo, here you go." He put the dog on the floor and urged him outside the bars into the corridor.

Milo stared at him.

"Keys, Milo. Go find the keys!"

Milo went into search mode, darting back and forth in the corridor.

One of the prisoners a couple of cells over said, "Jeezus. What was that just went running by? Was that a freakin' rat? They gotta get some traps in here!"

Stanley didn't want to distract Milo, so he eased back deeper into his cell, sat on the cot and prayed.

Milo came back, darted into the cell.

Dropped the guard's sandwich on the floor in front of Stanley's feet and wagged his tail.

"Oh, no. Not *cheese*. Keys. *Keys!*"

The dog cocked his head to one side.

"Go find the keys, boy!"

Milo yipped, darted out into the corridor.

The ice ages came and went, the universe ran down, time ended. . . .

Milo came back.

"All right! Good boy!" He grabbed the dog and hugged him.

Took the guard's keys from Milo's mouth.

Dorian's Cad arrived in front of the Coco Bongo, followed by two Chryslers full of his newly hired shooters. Searchlights painted the night sky, a crowd of tuxedoed and Armani-gowned socialites waited to be admitted. A banner over the front of the club proclaimed CASINO NIGHT CHARITY BALL. Reporters with floodlit minicams and popping 35mm cameras roamed about, took pictures.

Inside the Cad, Dorian wore a conservative black

silk tux with diamond studs. Next to him, Tina wore a slinky, fit-like-paint off-the-shoulder black & red evening gown and matching six-inch heels, courtesy of the mask. The mask, which now sat in his lap, despite his resolve earlier to keep it on. He'd gotten so tired all of a sudden he just had to have a break. A minute to gather himself, that was all he needed, and *then* he'd take care of business.

Tina started to light a cigarette.

Dorian grabbed it, crushed it between his fingers. "Let's don't start the celebration until afterward, hey? Besides, carelessness with fire could be dangerous."

He waved at the crates on the floor under his feet. They were marked C-7 USMC DEMOLITION MATERIALS: DANGER!

He had conjured them out of nothing while wearing the mask.

This was going to be sommme fun.

"Showtime, folks," Dorian said. He smiled at Tina.

Raised the mask.

Stanley didn't much like guns, but the one in the guard's holster was right there and just getting out of the cell and this section of the jail might be the easiest part of this whole thing. Reluctantly, he unsnapped the holster's strap and eased the revolver out. He didn't plan to use it, but if they thought he might, that could help. With any luck at all, he could sneak out of the police station without any-

body noticing him at all and be gone before anybody realized it.

He began to back away, but the guard's snores
choked off as something woke him. He sat up, saw
Stanley, and came out of the chair, reaching for his
gun at the same time. Came up empty, which
slowed him down long enough for Stanley to step
to the side and swing the gun. He hit the guard up-
side the head and the man groaned and fell.
Sprawled flat out on his face.

Milo howled.

Stanley said, "Sorry, man, but I have to to get
out of here."

A couple of the prisoners started yelling. "Hey,
what's going on out there?"

Stanley looked around. Couldn't see his dog.
"Milo? Where are you?"

The dog whimpered.

"Milo!"

Stanley grabbed the guard and pulled on him.
Milo was under the stunned man.

"Milo! You okay?"

The dog wagged his tail. Apparently so.

"Hey!" a prisoner said.

"Everybody shut up!" Stanley ordered. He
waved the gun.

Everybody shut up.

How about that? It was true: you could get more
with kind words and a gun than you could with
kind words alone—well, if *shut up* could be considered kind.

He turned and headed for the door past the guard's station.

The door opened and Kellaway stepped inside.

Wasn't that just great?

"Ipkiss!"

"You don't want to make any sudden moves there, Lieutenant. I mean, I'm seriously stressed out here, and God knows what might happen." He waved the revolver. He wasn't even sure how to shoot it, if it had a safety or anything. But nobody knew he didn't know that, either.

"Take it easy, Stanley. How did you get out of your cell? Where did the dog come from—?"

"Never mind. We've got to get to the Coco Bongo Club, fast."

"Not a chance, you idiot. We're in the middle of a police station. You think you can just waltz out all by yourself?"

Stanley thought about it for a second. "No. You're probably right. I can't. But *we* can, Lieutenant. Ease your gun out, carefully, use two fingers."

Kellaway said, "Shows what you know. I had to check it to get into the jail."

"Fine. What about your cuffs?"

Kellaway tendered those.

Stanley handcuffed his left wrist to Kellaway's right wrist.

"What are you doing?"

"I can't leave by myself, but I can as your prisoner." He put the gun into the front of his shirt, as if he were scratching his belly like Napoleon. "Don't do anything stupid."

"You know what happens to cop killers, Stanley? Shoot me and they will tear you limb from limb."

"Probably, but you won't live to be smug about it, now, will you?"

"What about the dog?"

"What about him? This is a police station, they've seen weirder things than a dog, haven't they?"

Kellaway shook his head. "This is crazy, Ipkiss. You're just getting in deeper."

"If I don't get out of here and to the club, it won't matter how deep I get. Move."

Stanley didn't feel particularly tough or brave, but he knew he had to do something or Tina was going to get hurt. He couldn't let that happen, no matter what happened to him.

They started walking.

The carhop hustled toward the Cad, thinking of his tip, no doubt.

Dorian/Mask laughed. Blew the doors right off the Cad. The driver's door missed the hop by six inches.

"Holy God!" he said.

"Close," Dorian/Mask said as he leaped from the car in a flare of blinding pyrotechnics and landed next to the carhop. "But you can call me The Man! Ta-dah!"

He threw his arms wide. Lightning forked the clear sky and thunder boomed. The searchlights changed so that each one now emitted a full rainbow spectrum.

Dorian/Mask said, "Excuse me, sonny." Then he threw a triple back layout somersault with two full twists over the top of the Cad and landed in front of Tina's door. Extended his arm.

Tina alighted from the doorless Cad and nervously took his arm.

"Shall we go in, my dear?"

The crowd stood back in awe. Dorian/Mask waved his free hand and four cupidlike nymphs materialized, each with a basket full of rose petals. The four danced back and forth in front of Dorian/Mask and Tina, strewing the roses in their path as they walked toward the front entrance.

Dorian/Mask nodded and spoke to the crowd. "So nice to see you. Hello. How are you? How's the wife? Glad you could make it."

Somebody popped a flashbulb.

"Please, no pictures. You'll mess up my concentration."

He waved again. Each camera in the crowd morphed, turned into a live snake. Boa constrictors, king snakes, pythons, cobras, a couple of leopard snakes thrown in for color.

Reptiles were dropped with a maximum of surprise and exclamations. And the crowd scrambled to get away from the squirming beasts.

Dorian/Mask looked over his shoulder at Sweet

and Orlando and the shooters. "Don't forget to bring the party favors, boys. Nothing like a little fireworks to liven up a dull party, hey?"

Gonna be a hot time in the old town to-nnniiiight!

They were going down the steps somewhat stiffly, Stanley knew, but so far so good. A couple of cops had even bent to pet Milo as he passed.

A plainclothes cop stood next to a patrol car parked in front of the precinct, eating a doughnut. Doyle, Stanley recalled.

"Hiya, Loot. Where you taking Ipkiss?"

Stanley decided to try and put a little shine on the counterfeit coin he was trying to pass. "It's a bum rap, I tell you. You really have the wrong guy. Ow! Take it easy, you're breaking my arm."

Doyle swallowed a mouthful of the cruller. "Hey, Lieutenant, don't give him any reason to sue us, okay?"

"My lawyer will have your badge," Stanley said. They kept moving.

Kellaway smiled at Doyle. "Ixnay! E-hay's ot-gay an-hay un-gay—ow!"

Stanley jammed the gun's barrel into Kellaway's ribs, hard.

Doyle smiled. "Hey, pig latin! I haven't heard that since I was a kid!"

If looks were knives, Doyle would have been flensed like a sailing ship full of whalers doing a great blue. Stanley whispered, "Keep moving."

"Hey, look a dog. Oh, lemme try it. Eee-say oo-yay ater-lay, oot-lay." He grinned.

"Idiot," Kellaway said.

"There's a car right over there," Stanley said. "Let's go for a ride. You drive."

Wheezing, Milo ran up behind them.

"You're making a mistake, Ipkiss. This is kidnapping. After your twenty in the local pen, the feds'll get you for another twenty."

"It doesn't matter. If we don't get to the club, my only reason for living will probably be gone anyhow. Move."

They moved.

15

The inside of the club had been transformed into a full-scale casino for the event, no expense spared. There were roulette wheels, crap tables, slot machines, imported from the Swede's operations in Monte Carlo and Vegas. In the middle of the main room, floating almost twenty feet up on nearly invisible wires, was a giant Plexiglas piggy bank, half-full of cash, with an electronic thermometer next to the bank that showed they'd already raised more than a hundred grand for charity. Hundreds of people worked the machines and tables while a girl in a little spangled leotard up on a tall stepladder dumped yet more bills into the piggy from a golden bucket marked with dollar signs.

Well. Wasn't this all just too cute?

Dorian/Mask entered the room, and the gamblers were so intent on their business hardly anybody noticed.

Just inside the entrance, some wannabe cool guy pulled a drink from a passing tray and turned around to hit on the cigarette girl.

Dorian/Mask watched the dude.

"Hello, there, tall, blond, and beautiful. That's a lovely outfit you're almost wearing. Did I mention I was a war orphan?"

The girl rolled her eyes. "You want something, sir?"

"Oh, but yes. Bliss. Passion. To have your children."

"I have plain, filtered, menthol, and cigars. That's all I'm selling here."

"What a pity."

She shook her head. Walked away.

He'd seen the dude somewhere before. Probably came into the club with the other wannabes, paid the bouncer fifty bucks, and then mingled with the VIPs who waltzed in for free.

Where had he ?

Oh, yeah. The bank. This was the guy who had been sitting next to Ipkiss when Tina had done the recon. Ah, well. Timing was everything. This guy had picked the wrong night to try to score in the Coco Bongo.

A woman wearing way too much makeup and a very scary wig shoved the dude aside. Damned if *she* didn't look familiar, too. He had a good memory for faces. Where . . . ?

Hey! It was the dragon in the apartment building. With the flamethrowing shotgun!

The woman said to the wannabe, "Outta my way, buster. Mama feels lucky tonight." The dude who'd been trying to make time with the cigarette girl turned. "Mrs. Peenman?"

"Do I know you?"

"I'm a friend of Stanley's."

"Leave me alone, you creep, or I'll call security! Ipkiss is crazy, and come the first, he's out of my building!"

She must not listen to the news, Dorian/Mask thought. Ipkiss was going to spend the next twenty years in stir. Too bad he couldn't be here, that would have really made it old home week, wouldn't it?

A reporter waving a mike went past Dorian/ Mask, stopped, and stared at him for a second, then remembered he had another goal. The reporter worked his way through the crowd toward a clot of overdressed people, in the middle of which was the mayor of Edge City.

The mayor was talking to the Swede. Thick as thieves, they were, which was the truth. Birds of a feather.

The reporter said, "Mr. Mayor, any words for our audience?"

"Why, certainly. I would like to thank all the citizens of Edge City who have come out to support this charity. We hope to raise a lot of money here tonight, and I hope everybody has a great time doing it."

Dorian/Mask took a deep breath. People around him staggered from the sudden disappearance of available oxygen. Hot damn! To Tina, he said, "You wait right here. I need to go have a word with the Swede. Or something."

She nodded dumbly.

Dorian/Mask strode across the floor as if he owned it. Which, when you got right down to it, he did. He owned the whole damned city, or would shortly.

The Swede's bodyguards saw him coming and moved to stand in his way.

Behind him, Dorian/Mask's boys began to filter into the room. He was aware of this because he now had eyes in the back of his head.

Dorian/Mask stopped and grinned his wicked grin. Waved at the guards. Atlas and Goliath's eyes rolled back in their respective heads and they both fainted.

The Swede looked over at him. Frowned. "Who the hell are you?"

Dorian/Mask gave him a military bow. "My, how fast they forget. Your favorite employee for years and years and now you don't know me?"

The Swede's frown increased. "Tyrel? What are you doing with that stupid costume on?"

"Payback, Swede." He turned, saw his gunners. Yelled. "Okay, boys, hit it!"

The gunners drew weapons from under their tuxedos. Started blasting.

"Jesus!" the Swede yelled. "Boys!"

His own men, scattered through the club, pulled their pieces and opened up.

The crowd went wild.

Armani and Kamali and Givenchy worth tens of thousands hit the floor as the wearers dropped flat, heedless of their expensive outfits. The air was filled with real heavy metal, lead and copper and brass, booms followed by singing like crazed bees.

Slot machines shattered and shat coins; lights exploded; screams rose and fell in surflike waves, soprano to bass.

Dorian/Mask grinned as the Swede emptied his piece into him from ten feet away, fifteen rounds of 9mm from his gold-plated Taurus PT–92. The bullets hit him, sank in, but didn't hurt a bit.

The Swede's pistol ran dry. He ejected the magazine, shoved in a replacement, started shooting again.

Dorian/Mask blew on his fingernails and polished them on his jacket, absorbing the bullets. This time, after half a dozen rounds did no damage, the Swede must have figured Dorian was wearing Kevlar, so he aimed for the head. He pumped the last nine shots into the mask. One even hit his eye with a squishy thump.

The Swede finished off the second magazine and stood there, amazed. As he ran empty, so did most of the other shooters. The place got very quiet.

Everybody left standing was a player, all the citizens were on their bellies or out the door by now.

"You all done?" Dorian/Mask said.

The Swede stared at him, stunned to amazed silence.

Dorian/Mask took a deep breath, puffed his cheeks out as if he were going to spit. . . .

He sprayed bullets from his mouth with machine-gun speed and velocity, complete with explosive sound effects.

He stitched a line across the Swede's thick chest. The man stumbled backward.

Dorian/Mask expectorated more death, crisscrossed the stunned man with lines of impact. Blew him backward and off his feet. The Swede flew through the air, hit the wheel of fortune, and stuck, like an apple thrown onto a bed of sharp nails. The wheel turned slowly, one revolution, two. Stopped with the pointer at "Lose Everything."

"Amen," Dorian/Mask said. "Next, anybody?"

Inside the police car, Stanley said, "Faster!"

He had uncuffed himself from Kellaway, but sat on the front seat with the gun jammed into the cop's side. He had carefully buckled his seat belt but made Kellaway keep his off. If the lieutenant thought to slam on his brakes suddenly, he was the one going through the windshield, not Stanley.

"You're crazier than a shithouse rat, you know that, Ipkiss? By the time you get out of jail, those *clothes* will be in style again. We'll have people living on Mars."

"If anything happens to Tina, it won't matter. Faster."

The car Dopplered through an intersection, skidded slightly as Kellaway swerved to avoid plowing into a van, then straightened out.

"You're a pretty good driver," Stanley said.

"Thanks. I won top gun at the LEOA's annual competition."

Dorian/Mask walked to where Tina lay. He grabbed her wrist with one hand and jerked her to her feet. "Orlando, show these nice people how we do piñatas around here."

Orlando nodded, pointed his piece at the Plexiglas pig overhead, and opened up on it. The pig shattered and an avalanche of green bills and shiny plastic shards fell on the crowd.

The shooters ran around with garbage bags, scooping the cash up.

"Now, isn't this fun? Uh, folks, we'd like to have wallets and jewelry to go along with the cash. Just hand them to the ushers, please."

It wasn't like he needed the money. It was just too cool *not* to do it.

The police car cut its lights and siren and rounded the corner close to the Coco Bongo. It glided to a stop.

People streamed from the club like panicked insects from a stepped-on anthill.

Stanley said to Kellaway, "There's no safety on this thing, right? You just point it and pull the trigger?"

"Jesus. I can't believe this. You think I would help you shoot somebody?"

"Suit yourself. I'm gonna take the keys and leave you handcuffed to the steering wheel, but you can use the radio, right?"

"Excuse me?"

"The radio. To call for help. Backup. We're going to need it."

"Ipkiss, what the hell are you talking about?"

"The Mask. He's in there and he's probably going to destroy the place and kill everybody inside."

"Christ, you expect me to believe—"

"I don't care what you believe, Lieutenant. Dorian Tyrel is The Mask and he's in there. He's got Tina."

He turned to the dog, sitting happily on the backseat. "You stay here, Milo. It's going to be dangerous and I don't want you to get hurt. Stay, boy, okay?"

The dog wagged its tail.

Stanley handed Kellaway the handcuffs. "To the steering wheel."

The Lieutenant obeyed. "You really going after Tyrel?"

"Yeah."

"No safety on the piece. Just point it and pull the trigger."

"Thanks. So long, Kellaway. If I don't come back, see that Milo gets a good home, would you? He's a really good dog."

With that, he opened the passenger door and slid out. He gripped the gun tightly and started for the club's entrance.

This was probably not the brightest thing he'd ever done. In fact, it probably ranked right up there with thinking he'd won ten million dollars when he'd gotten that envelope from Publisher's Clearing House, or maybe the time he'd thought he could fly if he said "Shazam," then jumped off the roof of his house and broke his arm.

But if Tina was in there and Tyrel had her, he had to go and get her. He'd never be able to live with himself, even in jail, if he didn't try.

He took a deep breath and blew it out. Time to see what you're really made of, Stanley.

16

There was a waterfall near the kitchen, complete with a twelve-foot-tall copy of the club's logo, the stylized monkey playing a bongo drum in the branches of a coconut palm, all in multicolored neon.

Dorian/Mask dragged Tina through the waterfall's pond to the neon tree and shoved her against it.

"Hey—!"

"Shut up, Tina." He waved his hands. Seaweed rose from the pond and twined itself around her, lashing her to the tree.

"Dorian, c'mon, this isn't funny!"

"What? Of course it's funny. This is your big production number, baby. You get to go out with a bang."

He waved at the shooters, led by Sweet and Or-

lando. They were stacking boxes of the explosive
he'd had in the Cad all over the interior of the club.
Yessir, the Swede would have the place all to himself
real soon now and to hell with it. With the money
he had and the mask, who needed any of this? It
ought to make a nice fireworks display. The perfect
way to top off a perfect evening, no?

He took a big glob of the plastic explosive and
pressed it against the tree next to Tina. Grinned as
he shoved a small electronic timer into the plastique
and started the countdown. "Bye-bye your life, bye-
bye," he said. "Give my regards to the Swede when
you see him, hey?"

When Stanley sneaked in through the rear entrance, the first person he saw was Charlie. Maybe
two dozen of the club's patrons crouched behind
food containers and trash cans and appliances,
afraid to move. Charlie had one arm each around
a waitress and a cigarette girl. He was obviously
frightened, but not so much so he couldn't take advantage of the opportunity to try to make time with
the two scared women.

"So what's your sign? Me, I'm a—Stanley? What
are *you* doing here?"

"She came in with that . . . thing," Charlie said.
"When the shooting started, I, ah, helped the girls
here escape to the kitchen. As far as I know, Tina
was still in there when it all died down."

"You've got to get these people out of here,
Charlie. There's no telling what the guy in the mask

might do, he could blow this whole place away with a wave of his hand."

"That's crazy—"

"The way I came in is clear. Back there."

"But—but what if we run into one of those thugs? I mean, ah, I don't want anything to happen to Daisy and Ariel here."

Stanley shook his head. "Here." He handed Charlie the gun he'd taken from the guard at the jail. "Just point this at anybody who gets in your way and pull the trigger until they move. Easy."

"Gee, Stan—"

"Do it, Charlie. I don't have time to debate about it."

Charlie sighed and nodded. "Okay, girls, you heard the man. Time to leave. Stay behind me." He waved the gun.

Stanley looked at him. With any luck, maybe he wouldn't blow his own foot off or shoot any of the other patrons.

Charlie moved away, waving at the others hiding in the kitchen. They followed him toward the exit.

Stanley, meanwhile, worked his way toward the club's main room. There was a short corridor leading from the kitchen and he moved down it slowly. A pair of in-and-out doors lay at the end of the corridor. He pushed the out door open a crack, peeped in.

The place was a wreck. Coins lay all over the floor like silver dust bunnies; shattered gambling equipment—slot machines, roulette wheels, like that—also lay dead or mortally wounded on the floor. Along with several thugs. A pall of blue smoke obscured things, and the air smelled like burned electrical wiring. Some party. It looked like *Bad Day at Black Rock* out here. And he hoped he wasn't Spencer Tracy.

. He eased into the room. The smoke was thick enough so he couldn't see all that much. If Tina were in here, he'd have to go find her—

Two things happened at once: he felt a cold metal finger poke him at the base of his skull and a voice said, "Don't even breathe funny, pal."

Uh-oh.

The metal touch went away and the voice—it sounded familiar —said, "Turn around. Real slow."

He did.

It was Orlando. With a big pistol pointed at Stanley's eye. "Hey, Orlando. What's happenin', man?"

"Ipkiss? What are you doing here? You supposed to be in jail."

"The service was terrible. I checked out."

"Yeah, well, the boss is gonna be real happy to see you, I bet. Come on." He waved the gun.

Stanley saw Tina as Orlando marched him across the wreckage of what had been the Coco Bongo Club. She was tied to the neon palm tree with what looked like seaweed, in the little pond next to the club's waterfall.

More thugs made their way around on the floor,

scooping loose cash into bags or frisking a few of the partygoers who hadn't gotten out for their jewelry and wallets. Stanley thought he saw the mayor himself. A few of the thugs were stacking boxes or pressing lumps of what looked like putty against the walls and ceiling supports, and from what was stenciled on those boxes, it wasn't modeling clay. It was an altogether ugly scene. At the same time Stanley realized that while Dorian was homicidal, he didn't have a very good imagination. He was going to blow the place up with plastique? Jeez, how boring. He, Stanley, could do better than that if *he* were wearing the mask.

He repressed a shudder. Don't even *think* about putting that mask on again, Stanley.

"Look what I found, boss. A party crasher."

Dorian, wearing the mask, came out of the smoke.

"Well, well, well. Stanley. I thought they'd keep you in the slammer until they found a cure for jock itch. Come to save your girlfriend, eh? Look, just to show you there's no hard feelings, tell you what I'm gonna do—you two can spend the rest of your lives together, how's that? Of course, in your case, happily ever after is going to be about"—he slid his left sleeve aside to reveal a three-times-normal-size Rolex crusted with diamonds and rubies—"oh, about, three minutes. If my calculations are correct, Captain. And they always are, you know."

Tina smiled, but Stanley thought it was a sickly expression.

"Dorian. C'mon. It's you I'm crazy about."

"Really? Gee, that's too bad."

"C'mon, Dorian."

"Nope, you made your bed, now lie in it." He waved at the interior of the club.

"Can I ask a favor?"

"You can ask."

"One last kiss? Nobody kisses like you do, Dorian."

He gave her the shark smile. "That's true. Okay. I'm in a good mood." He moved toward her.

"Not with that thing on," she said. "From the real you."

"This is the real me."

"You know what I mean."

"Boss, shouldn't we be running along? All this explosive stuff is dangerous. And the clock is ticking."

"A few more seconds won't hurt anything," Dorian said. "Let me give the girl a final thrill before she goes to the Great Nightclub in the Sky."

He pulled the mask off. There came a hissing, popping noise. Tyrel morphed from what the mask made him back into his normal self. Not all that much different, when you got right down to it. Just a matter of degree.

Tyrel moved close to Tina, grinned, and laid a big one on her, pressing his open mouth against hers.

Her enthusiasm matched Tyrel's.

Stanley's heart shrank as he watched. Well. If

she could convince this maniac she loved him,
maybe he would let her go. That would be the important thing, even if Stanley didn't make it. Whatever it took.

Stanley saw the next part in a kind of slow
motion, as if time had suddenly turned thick and
syrupy:

Tyrel held the mask in his right hand, hanging
by his side as he kissed Tina roughly.

Tina drew her left foot back . . .

Kicked the mask . . .

The mask flew from Tyrel's hand . . .

Sailed high through the air, tumbling . . .

Sweet and Orlando turned to stare . . .

Tyrel jerked away from Tina and spun . . .

The mask fell toward the floor . . .

A small form hurtled through the air toward the
falling mask. . . .

Milo?

And time went back to normal speed as Milo
caught the mask as if it were a Frisbee and dropped
to the ground, the cursed bit of wood firmly in his
teeth. He started toward Stanley.

"Good boy!"

"Get that damned dog!" Tyrel yelled.

Orlando dived at Milo, missed.

Sweet gave it a shot, also missed, slid across the
floor on his face.

Now it was only Tyrel between Milo and Stanley. "C'mere, you ugly mutt! Gimme that!"

Milo dodged to the left, then right as Tyrel

lunged for him. It looked as if he were going to
make it—

Tyrel caught Milo's hind leg.

The dog yelped.

The mask fell from his grip.

Oh, no!

The mask hit the floor on its edge and bounced
like a basketball.

Milo jerked free of Tyrel's grip as the mask came
back down . . .

And landed squarely on the little dog's face.

Lightning flashed. Thunder boomed. Came the
whirlwind.

Tyrel said, "Oh, shit!"

Stanley watched, fascinated, as meek little Milo
transformed from an asthmatic mutt into Cerberus'
uglier brother. He had a giant green head with a
double row of jagged teeth. His cheap nylon collar
transformed, became covered with diamond studs.
His toenails extended into needle-sharp points
three inches long. His eyes glowed with green fire.
He turned toward the wide-eyed Tyrel and barked.
It sounded like a bomb going off, and the force of it
knocked Tyrel sprawling. He slid across the floor as
if shoved by a mighty hand. The rumble of Milo's
terrible *woof* blasted some of the more severely
wounded gambling equipment over with a series of
loud crashes.

"Good *boy!*" Stanley yelled.

Quickly, he turned toward Tina and began to
undo the seaweed that held her in place.

Behind him, he heard Tyrel screaming, "Get the dog!"

Stanley dug at the seaweed with frantic haste.

"Hurry up!" Tina said. "He's set a bomb with a timer on it."

"Where?"

"Behind me!"

He saw Milo go bounding past on his right, Sweet in pursuit. Milo stopped, so fast it looked as if he had taken root. Sweet skidded past the dog. Milo sank his teeth into Sweet's butt. Sweet howled. Milo shook him as if he were a mouse and tossed him halfway across the room, where he slammed into a huge slot machine. The machine began to flash lights and a siren.

Looked like Sweet had hit the jackpot.

The seaweed was slimy and hard to get a grip on. "Where's the bomb? I better shut it off first—"

He felt a hand on his shoulder. It spun him around. He had time to see Tyrel's face, lips peeled back in rage and hatred, before the man's fist smashed right into his forehead.

Stanley saw purple flashes as he fell back into the pond.

Tyrel came after him, trying to kick him while he was down. Fortunately, the water slowed his foot, and what he did was more splash than impact. Even so, it looked like the end of the trail. *Adios, amigos.* Say good night, Stanley, it's all over. . . .

Enough!

Stanley had had enough. The anger that only the

mask had been able to release, a lifetime of being trodden upon, all the crap for all the years, it boiled forth in a steaming red rage. This thug had tried to kill him, was trying to kill his woman!

This was not *right*!

He came to his feet, blocked the punch that Tyrel threw, and launched a fist of his own. It hit Tyrel squarely on the nose.

Tyrel went backward, probably more surprised than hurt, but that didn't matter.

Stanley went after him. He just had time for a flash of the action beyond Tyrel: Milo, now chasing Orlando, who was shooting over his shoulder at the dog to no effect whatsoever. Stanley managed a grin.

A mistake, that grin.

Tyrel came up and slammed into Stanley. They went down, Stanley on the bottom. Tyrel grabbed Stanley's throat with both hands. Stanley went under, hit the bottom of the shallow pool, hard. The hands tightened on his neck. The murky water filled his eyes. He couldn't breathe. Tyrel was straddling him, trying to kill him.

Stanley brought his knee up with all his strength. Hit the gangster in his most vulnerable spot, right between the legs.

Tyrel screamed, a high, girlish sound, and let go of Stanley's throat.

Stanley shoved at Tyrel's chest, got free of him, came up to his knees. Took a deep breath, got to his feet.

Tyrel stood hunched over, both hands clutching at his manhood.

Stanley stepped toward him.

Tyrel tried to straighten, to put his hands up.

Stanley laughed. Swung his right fist in an uppercut that started at the surface of the pond. Hit Tyrel under the chin. The man's teeth clacked together so hard the sound of it echoed in the big room.

Dorian Tyrel straightened out like a switchblade, arched backward, and hit the surface of the pond in a perfect back flop. Water splashed. Tyrel sank, then bobbed to the surface, arms outspread. Out cold.

Stanley looked at his fist in amazement. Then winced as the pain hit him. He rubbed at his injured fist with his other hand.

Milo/Mask flew through the air toward him. Stanley caught the dog and grinned at him. "Best dog in the world!" he said.

He pulled the mask from Milo's face. *Pop!* And the little dog was his normal self again.

A bullet cut the air two inches in front of Stanley's face. Another followed it. He jerked his gaze to the side, saw Sweet and Orlando and a couple of other thugs pointing their guns at him. "Drop it!" Orlando yelled.

Stanley instead dropped Milo, who splashed and bobbed to the surface in a quick dog paddle. He barked his happy bark: This is fun!

Another shot hit the mask and knocked it out of his hand. It sailed over the bar and out of sight.

The shooters ran toward it.

But Stanley was already sloshing across the pond, ahead of them. He cleared the water, leaped over the bar.

The shooters opened up. The bar filled with holes. The shooters fired until they ran empty.

And when it got quiet, The Mask stood up from behind the bar, hands outspread.

"Hey, hey, hey, boys and girls, I'm *back* and I'm beaaaauuutiful!"

17

Sweet and Orlando started frantically reloading. The other shooters stood there staring.

The Mask said, "Missed me, missed me, now you gotta kiss me!"

He picked up a drink from the bar top, a miracle the glass hadn't been hit, and took a long swig. Immediately he began to fountain from a dozen holes in his body. He looked like a sieve.

"Oops. Well, okay, so maybe you *don't* have to kiss me."

Orlando and Sweet dropped spare magazines in their haste to reload.

The Mask's expression went from smiling to grim. He reached into his pockets with both hands and came out with a dozen guns, barrels so long and huge he looked like a cartoon battleship.

"So, I gotta ask you one question. Do you feel lucky, punks? Well, do you?"

Sweet and Orlando didn't feel lucky, it seemed. They turned and ran.

"Stanley! The bomb!"

The Mask turned. Saw Tina strapped to the neon tree. Saw the bomb. The clock was flashing down. Four . . . three . . . two . . .

He zipped across the room in a blur. Grabbed the bomb, ripped it from where it was stuck, and with a mighty gulp, swallowed it. Smiled at Tina.

There was a muffled boom. His stomach ballooned out like a bullfrog's chin, five times its normal size. His pupils spun like slot-machine numbers. Smoke poured from his ears.

He tapped himself once on the chest with the top of his fist, turned away from Tina, and burped a fireball. Then blew a single, large smoke ring. Turned back to Tina. "Excuuuse me. That'sa some spicy meatball, you know?"

They smiled at each other. Then her eyes went wide. "Stanley! Behind you?"

The Mask turned. Saw Dorian splashing at him through the shallow water, a knife in his hand.

The Mask shook his head. "Guy doesn't know to quit when he's ahead, does he?"

The Mask turned back to the neon palm tree. Opened a hitherto hidden panel. Inside was a square of glass with a sign on it:

IN CASE OF EMERGENCY ONLY—BREAK GLASS.

The Mask said, "Hmm. I guess this qualifies as

an emergency. He hit the glass with his elbow. The cover shattered, revealing an old-fashioned white ceramic toilet-tank handle with the word PRESS imprinted on it. The Mask waggled his eyebrows at Tina, then grabbed the handle and pushed it down.

There came the sound of a giant toilet flushing.

Dorian slipped and fell to his knees. He started to get up, but stopped and stared as the water started to whirlpool around him. He started to spin, carried 'round and 'round in the whirlpool. Getting lower as the water level sank.

"Oh, shiiiiittttt!" he screamed as he and the water sank from sight.

The entire pond disappeared. There was a drain at the bottom the size of a manhole. It gurgled as the last of the water ran down it.

"Truer words were never spoken," The Mask said. He and Tina were left alone in the middle of the now dry pond. He pulled the mask from his face with a now familiar *pop!* He tore the last of the seaweed away from her, grabbed her, and kissed her. It was a four-star Technicolor smooch.

Off to the side, Milo barked.

The front door burst open and a squad of uniformed cops burst in, waving guns.

Stanley broke the kiss and looked over to see the cops. After a second Lieutenant Kellaway, accompanied by Charlie, followed them. As did Sweet and Orlando, in handcuffs.

Cops began grabbing the other thugs.

Kellaway started toward Stanley. "Party is over, Ipkiss. Come along."

A man in rumpled evening clothes moved to block Kellaway's path.

"Get out of my way, tubby—ah! Mr. Mayor?"

"That's right. What are you doing, Sergeant?"

"Uh, that's Lieutenant, sir."

"It is for now. Why are you threatening that young man?"

"He's The Mask."

"Nonsense. We all saw The Mask, he's Dorian Tyrel. That young man saved our lives."

"With a little help from his friends," Charlie said. He spun the gun Stanley had given him around his finger like a trick shooter.

The gun went off.

Almost everybody hit the floor.

Stanley took that moment to shove the mask under his shirt.

A uniform took the gun from Charlie.

"Sorry," he said.

"But—but—" Kellaway tried.

"But nothing. I didn't see it all, but what I did see was this man"—the mayor waved at Stanley—"as he fought with Tyrel and knocked him down."

Kellaway might not be the smartest cop in the world, but he knew better than to disagree with the man who hired the chief of police. He shook his head. "Okay. Whatever you say. Ipkiss is a hero and Tyrel is The Mask. Where is Mr. Tyrel, anyway?"

Stanley smiled. "I wouldn't worry about him. I think all his plans . . . went down the drain."

18

Charlie pulled his car to a stop on the Tahoochie Bridge. Dawn was about to break. He turned to Stanley and Tina. "You sure about this, pal?"

"I'm sure," Stanley said.

Stanley and Tina got out of the car.

From the backseat Milo barked happily at them.

Charlie shook his head. "What a waste."

Stanley and Tina walked over to the same spot where he'd first seen the mask in the water below. He leaned on the railing, held the mask out in space.

"Are *you* sure?" he said. "You aren't going to miss this guy?" He waved the mask. "All you'll be left with is me."

She smiled at him. Squeezed his arm. Reached over and knocked the mask out of his hand. It tumbled toward the water.

The two of them watched it fall, hit the water. Then they turned toward each other and embraced.

After a moment they broke the hug. Turned back toward the car.

"Hey, where's Charlie?"

Milo barked and ran to the edge of the bridge. Stanley turned back around. Looked down and saw Charlie floundering in the water. He was chasing the mask as it floated away. He did a belly flop as he lunged for it, but the wave from his body shoved the mask farther away from him. He sank, and by the time he came up from the murky river, the mask was beyond his reach.

"Rats!" he yelled.

On the bridge above him, Stanley and Tina laughed.

And watched as the mask floated away and out of their lives.

About the Author

STEVE PERRY has written dozens of science fiction and fantasy novels, the most recent of which is SPINDOC, along with several of the bestselling *Aliens*™ novelizations, alone and in collaboration with his daughter, Stephani. He has also written a number of animated teleplays, including among them several for the *Batman* series, as well as numerous short stories and articles. He lives in Beaverton, Oregon, with his wife, who publishes a small monthly newspaper.

From the author of the bestselling Amber series and from one of the genre's most popular humorists, a fantasy novel that posits that anything worth doing is worth doing well—especially if it's the end of the world...

BRING ME THE HEAD OF PRINCE CHARMING
Roger Zelazny and Robert Sheckley

Most people don't know the world ends every millennium. Generally nobody notices except for the forces of good and evil, who vie for control of the universe every thousand years.

Azzy Elbub, demon, is out to win the Millennial Evil Deeds Award for the year 1000, given to the being whose acts do the most toward reshaping the world. Azzy wants to create a "Frankenstein's hero" to send off on a doomed quest to wake up a sleeping princess. The plan, if it succeeds, will end with the princess stabbing her princely rescuer, then committing suicide—an evil deed indeed. Azzy is backed fully by the Powers of Darkness and is even given a credit card good for anything in Hell he might need. However, since he is competing for the Millennial Award, the Powers of Light are permitted to send an observer, and Azzy is stuck with the angel Babriel. And that's only the beginning of the end....

Bring Me The Head of Prince Charming
A rollicking romp through heaven and hell.